THE DOPEMAN'S BODYGUARD

Tranay Adams

Lock Down Publications and Ca$h
Presents

The Dopeman's Bodyguard

A Novel by *Tranay Adams*

Tranay Adams

Lock Down Publications
P.O. Box 870494
Mesquite, Tx 75187

Visit our website @
www.lockdownpublications.com

Copyright 2019 The Dopeman's Bodyguard

First Edition August 2019
Printed in the United States of America

This is a work of fiction. Names, characters, places, and incidents either are products of the author's imagination or are used fictitiously. Any similarity to actual events or locales or persons, living or dead, is entirely coincidental.

Lock Down Publications
Like our page on Facebook: Lock Down Publications @
www.facebook.com/lockdownpublications.ldp
Cover design and layout by: **Dynasty Cover Me**
Book interior design by: **Shawn Walker**
Edited by: **Kiera Northington**

Stay Connected with Us!

Text **LOCKDOWN** to 22828 to stay up-to-date with new releases, sneak peaks, contests and more...
Thank you.

Submission Guideline.

Submit the first three chapters of your completed manuscript to ldpsubmissions@gmail.com, subject line: Your book's title. The manuscript must be in a .doc file and sent as an attachment. Document should be in Times New Roman, double spaced and in size 12 font. Also, provide your synopsis and full contact information. If sending multiple submissions, they must each be in a separate email.

Have a story but no way to send it electronically? You can still submit to LDP/Ca$h Presents. Send in the first three chapters, written or typed, of your completed manuscript to:

LDP: Submissions Dept
Po Box 870494
Mesquite, Tx 75187

DO NOT send original manuscript. Must be a duplicate.

Provide your synopsis and a cover letter containing your full contact information.

Thanks for considering LDP and Ca$h Presents.

Acknowledgements

I would like to thank everyone that has purchased my novels, reviewed, and suggested them to a friend and / or has given me a shout-out. I greatly appreciate it. There are too many of you to name, so I hope this will suffice. Thank you a trillion timez for your support. I fuckz with chu the long way.

Special Shout Out!

Choc, Author Barbie Scott, Randy Coxton, Jane Pennella, Dorothea Creamer and Kim Leblanc.

This Book Is Dedicated To

Ethan (Alejandro) and Ayden (Garcia). I hope to have children just like you some day. Love your bestfriend, Nay.

Tranay Adams

CHAPTER ONE

King Rich moved down the hallway, moving the mop from left to right, cleaning the floor. Looking down at the linoleum, King Rich could see his reflection below him. King Rich was a baldheaded high-yellow man with a long, thick beard as white as snow. He stood a solid six-foot-two and had an athletic physique. He was in excellent shape for a fifty-nine-year-old man. King Rich was a self-made millionaire. He made his bones back in the sixties, taking hits on dope boys, leaving them lying face down with their dick in the dirt. Eventually, he hung up his guns and became what he hunted. Over time, his riches and power grew, which allowed him to expand his empire.

Hearing footsteps coming in his direction, he looked down the hallway to see four big, muscle bound niggaz headed his way. The one leading the pack, Death, had a mad-dog expression across his face and an ice pick-like shank in his hand. One of the goons with Death slid the corrections officer in the hallway something. Although King Rich didn't exactly see what it was, he was sure it was money because after the C.O., got it, he disappeared. He'd been paid off. King Rich didn't have to think about it, he already knew what these meat-headed niggaz were on. They were more than likely there on the behalf of Montray, who'd have sent them there to kill him.

Four...Four big, black, ugly mothafuckaz. I may be old, but I'm in shape. Let's just hope I'm in well enough shape to take 'em. Well, we're about to find out, King Rich thought as he unscrewed the end of the mop stick from its base, easily.

"What up, OG? You King Rich?" Death asked him as he hid the ice pick behind his leg. King Rich's eyes shot down to where Death had hidden the ice pick, then he looked him square in the eyes.

"Who's asking?" King Rich asked as he gripped the stick firmly with both hands.

"Montray wanted you to have this!" Death called out as he moved to jab King Rich in the heart with the ice pick. The ice pick had gotten halfway towards its mark, when King Rich swung the stick upwards and knocked it out of Death's hand. He then struck Death in the balls and swiftly swung the stick into his jaw, sending blood spraying from his mouth, which dotted up the wall. Death dropped to the floor, out of the fight. As soon as he did, King Rich roundhouse-kicked a second goon in the jaw, spilling him to the floor. He then kicked a third in the stomach, which doubled him over. King Rich followed up by swiftly swinging around and cracking him across the jaw with the stick. The fourth goon got jabbed in the stomach and then the throat with the stick, causing him to grab his neck and gag. King Rich then spun around and kicked the nigga in the chest. The impact from the blow lifted the last goon off his feet and sent him flying backwards. He landed on the wet floor and slid backwards on his back, eventually bumping up against the wall.

"Uhh!" King Rich hollered out as Death tackled him from behind and caused him to drop the mop handle to the floor. The brute lifted him over his head and dumped him on his back, causing him to bump his head. King Rich lay on the floor moaning, with his eyes rolled to the back of his head, barely conscious. While he lay there shocked, Death picked up his ice pick and straddled him. He grabbed him by the front of his uniform and brought the ice pick near his left eye.

"First, I'ma take yo eyeball outta ya fucking head, then I'm gonna kill ya!" a mean mugging Death assured an out-of-it King Rich. Death then bit down on his bottom lip and swung the ice pick downward. Before the tip of the prison-made blade could connect, a foot came out of nowhere, crashing underneath Death's chin. The blow lifted Death off of his feet and dropped him on his back. Death slowly lifted his head from the linoleum, dizzy, and looked down the hallway where the kick had come from. At first, he saw eight blurry individuals, but when his vision came back into place, he saw a total of four, hardcore gangsta Bloods. At the forefront was that nigga, Killa. He and all of his niggaz were strapped up with shanks.

Killa was a tall ass nigga who was the color of brass, and he wore his hair in pigtails on either side of his head. He had the state of California inked beside his right eye. In fact, his neck and hands were covered in jail house ink.

"What the fuck? Nigga, this ain't got nothing to do witchu!"

"It has everything to do with me!" a mean mugging Killa roared at him, like the beast the streets and the penitentiary had made him. "Take 'em all!"

Death's goons pulled out their shanks and they all locked ass with Killa and his goons. The sound of sharpened steel hitting warm flesh bounced off the walls and so did the screams of men in agony. Blood dotted up the walls and the floor, making it slippery. When the drama finally died down, Death's goons were lying on the floor, bleeding and hurting.

King Rich, who had just come to, rose from the floor, looking at all of the bodies lying twisted on the floor. Looking over his shoulder, he saw Killa'z goons standing around with blood dripping from their shanks. They watched as their leader, Killa, wiped his shank off on one of Death's goons and tucked it on his waistline. He then picked up the mop stick and strolled casually behind Death, who was crawling towards his ice pick, which was lying beside the mop bucket. Death reached for the ice pick and Killa swung the mop stick downward with all of his might. *Braaaack!* The end of the mop stick broke and Death slammed down into the floor, wincing.

"Aaaah! Aaaah, aaaah, aaaah!" Death hollered over and over again, teary-eyed, having felt a searing pain shoot through his back when the mop stick came down upon him. "Aaaaah, my back! My mothafucking back is broken! Aaaaah!"

"Shut cho bitch ass up, nigga! You know the life we chose. G.A.B.O.S.," Killa told him as he stood over him. "The Game Ain't Based On Sympathy."

Killa handed one of his goons the mop stick and then he grabbed Death by the back of his collar, dragging him over to the mop bucket. He dunked his head deep inside the murky, dirty water, causing bubbles to float up to the surface of the water. When he pulled Death out of the bucket, he gasped for air and pleaded for his life, but Killa wasn't trying to hear that shit. He dunked his bitch ass back inside the filthy water again. Again, bubbles floated to the surface of the water. Killa allowed Death to stay under the water a little longer each time he dunked his head inside the bucket. When Killa pulled Death's head out of the water the last time, he burped and gasped continuously for air.

"Please, please, no more! No more!" Death pleaded through narrowed eyelids, with dirty water dripping from his face and shit.

"Yeah, you right, no more of that! I got something else for yo hoe ass though!" Killa kicked the mop bucket over and spilled the murky water everywhere. He then looked to his goons and told them to pull Death's pants down around his ankles and to hold down his arms and legs. The goon he had given the mop stick to, gave it back to him and he and the rest of the goons did like they had been ordered to. "Yeah, hold his ass down just like that!" Killa harped up a glob of phlegm and spat it into the palm of his hand. He then stroked the mop stick up and down, lubricating it with his own spit. He then took hold of the stick with both hands and cocked it back at his side, in a ramming position. He had a wicked smile on his face and in his pupils, Death's flat, hairy ass cheeks as well as his asshole, flaccid dick and balls were reflected. Killa'z eyes were trained on Death's asshole. That's where he planned on putting the mop stick.

Death twisted and turned, squirming on the floor where Killa'z goons had him pinned down. A panicked expression was plastered on Death's face as he was trying his damndest to look over his shoulder to see exactly what Killa was doing with that mop stick, but he couldn't see him.

"What the fuck you gon' do with that, man?" Death hollered out, spit jumping from his big, fat lips.

"What chu think?" Killa asked him as he practiced ramming the mop stick up Death's ass.

"Aw, hell naw, dawg! Lemme go! Y'all can't do me like this, man! Lemme go!" Death hollered out. "Lemme g— Aaaaaaaaahhh!" Death's eyes nearly jumped out of his head and his mouth stretched all the way open, displaying every cavity inside. Veins bulged on his forehead, temples, and neck. He was so choked up from the mop stick slamming inside his butthole that he couldn't even scream. "Ack, ack, ack, ack, ahhh, ack, ack, ack!"

"Punk ass mothafucka!" Killa said as he fucked him up the asshole with the mop stick. Biting down on his bottom lip, he pulled the mop stick out of Death's hairy buttocks. The stick was covered in blood and had speckles of shit on it. The smell of shit impregnated the air. All King Rich could do was frown up and shake his head, seeing how Killa was doing the man that had tried to take his life. He didn't feel sorry for him though. Hell naw! What the fuck he looked like feeling sorry for the mothafucka that tried to snatch him out of the world. "How'd you like that, gorgeous? Huh? How you like that? You want some more? Huh? You want some more?"

"No, man, please! I'm sorry, dawg. I'm sorr— aaaaaahh!" Death hollered out again, eyes bulging and mouth hanging open. His eyes were red webbed and tears were running from them, sliding down his cheeks. "Ack, ack, ack!" He became choked up again, feeling the mop stick up his asshole, splitting his booty hole wide open and causing more blood and shit to run up out of him.

"Fuck a sorry, nigga! Yo ass gon' learn today!" Killa swore to Death. He yanked the mop stick out of Death's butthole and with a grunt, rammed that mothafucka back up in him. From the brutality he inflicted on the man, anyone looking on at him would have sworn he was a straight-up savage. And he was.

Killa yanked the mop stick out of Death and the nigga farted. Killa walked around Death and kicked him in his side. He then ordered his goons to hold the nigga'z head up. When the goons held Death's head up, his eyes were rolled to their whites and his mouth was hanging open as he moaned in pain. Killa gripped the mop stick with both hands and swung it like a baseball bat across Death's jaw. What was left of the mop stick broke in half and Death's face slammed to the floor. He was knocked out cold!

Breathing huskily, Killa wiped his fingerprints off the half of the mop stick that was left and dropped it to the floor. He then walked over to King Rich and introduced himself, shaking his hand.

14

"...Your son hired me to be your bodyguard in here. During the duration of your stay at this lovely correctional facility, me and my niggaz will watch over you. Lemme introduce you to 'em." Killa turned around to his goons and introduced them to King Rich, one by one. He then turned back around to King Rich. "From now on, you're sticking with us, we move as a unit. Cool?" he held out his balled fist for some dap.

"Cool." King Rich dapped him up.

"Good. Come on." He tapped King Rich and motioned for him to follow him and his goons as they mobbed up the hallway, leaving Death and his battered goons behind.

Six months later

"I'm fucked, Rich. I mean, I'm really, really fucked, Blood," Killa told King Rich as he walked beside him on the track. Killa had been down for two murders, which he'd caught during a drive-by shooting. He was given life without the possibility of parole, but he had appealed his case.

"Talk to me. What's on yo mind, son?" King Rich asked the twenty-seven-year-old Killa, with a concerned expression on his face. King Rich was in a heated war over drug territory with a ruthless gangsta by the name of Montray. Montray couldn't get his hands on King Rich in the streets, so he blackmailed his chauffeur into planting a murder weapon inside his vehicle. This landed him behind the concrete walls and barbwire fences of the correctional facility. Montray figured since he had so many connections behind the wall, the kingpin would be easier to get, which was why he set him up. As soon as King Rich got behind bars, he had killaz on his head, on behalf of Montray. So, he'd hired a notorious killer of his own behind the wall as his bodyguard, a top-ranking Blood gangbanger, Killa, who was from the Eastside Outlaw Rolling Twenties Blood gang. It was said that Killa was highly skilled in Ninjutsu, and had killed more men than he could count on both his hands and feet, allegedly.

Killa stopped walking and looked King Rich in the face, on the verge of tears. "They denied my appeal. You know what that means? I'm going to spend the rest of my life in here with these mothafuckaz, Blood!" When he said this, King Rich looked off into the yard at all the rest of the convicts going on about their business. He then looked into the troubled eyes of his bodyguard, listening to the rest of what he had to say to him. "I did a lotta wicked shit in my life but damn, to go out like this, rotting behind these fucking walls. I'd rather not, man. I couldn't hack it. I couldn't take it, G." Tears broke down Killa'z cheeks and he wiped his eyes with the back of his hand. For the first time in his life, King Rich saw a gangsta cry.

King Rich stood there looking at Killa, not knowing exactly what to say to him. He knew that no matter how emotionless a man was, he was still human and in being human, the thought of spending your natural life behind bars was a bitch. Although the life he and Killa chose paved only two roads, death or jail, it was still a hard pill to swallow once the shit happened. It was like Nas once said, "Life is a bitch and then you die." *Damn!*

"Niggaz always talking about killing yo self is the coward's way out, but fuck them, Blood. What the fuck do they know about niggaz like you and me? I've had it hard my entire life! Group homes, molestation, getting shot, stabbed, losing my son and countless homies to this gang shit! Now, I'm told I've gotta spend the rest of my fucking life in this shithole? Nah, man, I can't get with that! I can't go out like that, my nigga. You feel me?" He sniffled and wiped his dripping eyes again with the back of his hand.

"Yeah, I feel you, young homie! Here." King Rich pulled a rag out of his back pocket and gave it to Killa, urging him to wipe his eyes. "Gone and dry yo eyes. You don't want these fools to see you out here like this. You know word travels fast and I know you not tryna tarnish yo reputation."

"I'm good, Blood, fuck these niggaz! I'm the biggest, baddest guerilla on this compound. And I dare a nigga to challenge that, onna gang!" Killa threw up the Bloody B, three fingers extended with his index and thumb forming the letter, O.

King Rich nodded and tucked his rag back where he'd pulled it out from. "I feel you, homie. What chu gon' do though?"

"I'll tell you what I'm gon' do. Fuck God! I'ma take my destiny into my own hands, boss dawg." Killa smiled at him devilishly as teardrops fell from his eyes. He then pulled out a pencil with a razor attached to it. The sunlight bounced off of it and the small metal rectangle gleamed.

"What the fuck?" King Rich's eyes bulged as the gleam reflected off his face. "You're not thinking about offing yo self or you?" he looked up into Killa'z eyes and saw emptiness like he always had. The man was a coldblooded killer that didn't give a mad ass fuck about nothing or no one that wasn't near and dear to him.

"That's exactly what I'm going to do, G." Killa told him, looking insane as a mothafucka with a tear drenched face and a creepy smile across his face.

"My nigga, I can't let chu—" King Rich went to grab Killa'z arm and he sliced him across his hand, causing him to holler out in agony and grab his dripping hand.

"Don't chu try to stop me, Rich, man! I'll kill you! I'ma nigga that doesn't have nothing to lose and that's the worst kinda nigga to fuck with!" He pointed the razor at him threateningly before retreating back to the yard. King Rich watched in horror as Killa ran past hittas that had once tried to off him on Montray's behalf, slicing some of them across the face and others across the throat. Their blood sprayed anyone standing next to them. Some of them bugged their eyes and grabbed the slit in their neck. Their blood coated the collar of their uniforms and they blinked uncontrollably before falling to the ground.

The guard hollered from the tower, "Get down, get down!" By this time, inmates were scattering and diving to the dirt. While they were doing that, Killa had his eyes set on a female corrections officer. She was a skinny white chick with ocean blue eyes and her hair pulled back in a bun. She went to draw down on a rampaging Killa, but he kicked her in the stomach, doubling her over. When she went to point her gun, Killa kicked it out of her hand and it spun around in circles as it flew across the sky. Killa then punched her in the jaw and grabbed her, pulling her into him with her back against him. Using one hand, he pulled the female corrections officer's head to the side, which exposed the bulging vein in her neck. He then brought the razor toward her throat as her terrified eyes watched the deadly blade come across her line of vision.

Killa looked up into the tower and saw the marksman setting up to shoot him. He smiled to himself, thinking it was almost over. The entire time, his plan had been for him to commit suicide. He felt like this was the best way, because he couldn't find the courage to off himself. And, on top of that, the nigga wanted to go out with a bang. This way, he was sure his death would be talked about for years and years to come. He'd already been a legend in the streets. This would make sure he died a legend in prison. *Come on, come on! Hurry up so we can get this shit over with!* Killa thought, seeing the marksman aim at him. "See ya, gorgeous." Killa kissed the female corrections officer on the side of the head and swiped the razor across her throat. A large slit opened on her neck and blood sprayed out crazily. The woman's eyes were as big as saucers and she gagged. Killa released her body and watched it drop to the ground. He then took the liberty to spit on it and then kick it. "Cracka ass bitch, I never liked yo uppity ass no way!"

All of the convicts were lying on the ground except for Killa. He was standing with his arms spread, blood staining his face, uniform and hands. He looked up at the sunny sky, watching the birds fly across his line of vision. Killa took one last deep breath of fresh air as a living man, a smile accenting his face. He brought his head down and locked eyes with the marksman who had just chambered a jacketed round inside his rifle.

Plowl!

The round sounded off loud and dangerously. And then it happened, the side of Killa'z head exploded and his lifeless body dropped to the ground. He lay on his back with half of his melon missing, staring at King Rich and wearing a smile on his face. King Rich shut his eyelids and shook his head, hating to see someone so young have their life taken.

Damn!

***

King Rich made his way inside the visitors' room, along with all of the other inmates. One by one, the convicted felons located their families and went to meet up with them. King Rich stood where he was, scratching the side of his face, looking all around for his son. Across the room he spotted his boy, twenty-seven-year-old, Baby Boy. He was a short, big head, light-skinned nigga that rocked his golden brown hair in six neat cornrows. He had beady eyes, a big nose and a goatee outlined his jaw and mouth flawlessly. At the moment, he was dressed in a white suit and an Easter pink tie and button down shirt. The young man that King Rich was grooming to take over his empire rose to his feet once he laid eyes on his father. King Rich and Baby Boy embraced one another, patting each other on their back.

"Good to see you, Pop," Baby Boy told his father after sitting down.

"Good to see you too, son," King Rich replied before clearing his throat with his fist to his mouth.

"How're you holding up?"

"Let's just say if it wasn't for me being in shape at my age, I'd surely be dead."

Baby Boy frowned up and said, "It's that bad? What happened to homie we got to hold you down up in here?"

"They killed Killa," he informed him, then went on to tell him exactly how Killa committed suicide.

"Damn." Baby Boy took a breath and ran his hand down his face. He looked stressed out now and truthfully, he was. He loved his father and he didn't want anything to happen to him while he was behind the wall. If something did, then he knew he'd go crazy. "What about the crew that was backing 'em?"

"Please, they didn't want no smoke with the cats up in here," he explained to him. "As soon as that boy's body dropped, I was sent a kite saying I was on my own. It seems as though they didn't have no heart unless Killa was backing nem."

"Pussy-ass niggaz, pardon my language, Pop."

"It's okay, son." He patted his youngest boy on the hand. "Don't chu worry, Pop, I'ma make some phone calls and see who I can get to hold you down up in here."

"Okay." He nodded his head, having full confidence that his son would find someone to have his back for as long as he was on lock.

Once the visit was over, King Rich and Baby Boy gave one another a manly hug. Then, they parted ways.

***

"Look, I don't mean to be all up in yo business, but why are these fools tryna take yo head? What chu do to have 'em on yo ass like that?" Latrell asked King Rich from where he was lying stretched out on the bottom bunk, picking the dirt from his nails. He and King Rich had been cellmates since the OG had touched down. Out in the yard they didn't talk much, but once they were in the confinement of their cell, they chopped it up like a couple of old high school buddies. They got along exceptionally well, but Latrell made sure he stayed out of the man's personal affairs. As far as he was concerned, he was getting out in less than a year on a robbery charge and he wasn't trying to fuck that up for nobody. Still, he had mad love for the old man. He looked at him like an uncle and shit.

"This beef is over drug territory." King Rich gave him the cold, hard truth. "Knock off the head and the body must follow. Least that's what I think my rival, Montray, be-lieves." He was speaking about his enemy trying to get him

21

hit while he was inside the prison. It was crazy, because Montray was trying to get King Rich knocked off while he was on lock and King Rich's people were trying to knock his head off in the streets.

"Niggaz is playing chess, not checkers, huh?" Latrell massaged his chin as he thought on it.

"Yeah, the son of a bitch couldn't manage to get me on the streets, so he had my chauffeur plant a gun in the car, which landed me in here. I guess he figured I'd be easier to hit while inside."

King Rich and Latrell went about chopping it up the remainder of the night until they both eventually fell asleep.

CHAPTER TWO

The mess hall was alive with chit chatter and convicts stuffing their faces with the slop the state dared to call food. Latrell sat across from King Rich having a casual conversation, while keeping his eyes on everything surrounding them. He had to keep his eyes peeled at all times because the last thing you wanted to happen was to get caught lacking, especially in a place as chaotic as prison.

"I can't eat any more of this bullshit. I'ma go dump my tray," King Rich told Latrell, before rising from where he was perched on the bench with his tray of food. Latrell gave him a nod as he continued to eat from his tray. King Rich walked across the mess hall toward the trash can and got purposely bumped by another inmate, which caused him to drop his tray. Some of the food that was left on his tray splashed and dotted his pants leg, which caused him to frown up and look down at it. He then looked up at the man that had bumped into him. "Say, bruh, why don't chu watch where you're going?"

"Nah, you old bitch, you watch where you're going!" The inmate swung a shank at King Rich's head. He ducked him, jumped back and kicked him in the stomach, which made him double over. King Rich then whacked him in the back of the head, dropping him to the floor. King Rich's eyes darted to their corners as someone ran at him, with a long ass shank. He spun around on his toes, blocking the wild swings of his attacker's weapon with his cane, gracefully.

"I'm gonna kill you, man! I'm gonna punch your old ass fulla holes, nigga!" King Rich's attacker swore up and down, swinging the shank consistently like a sword.

"I hear you talking, youngsta, but chu gon' have to make this old timer a believer." King Rich scowled, fully prepared for whatever threat his attacker posed.

The attacker came at King Rich, swinging the shank crazily. The kingpin dodged the blade easily as agile as a gymnast. The attacker swung the shank once more and it sliced through King Rich's uniform shirt, leaving a thin bloody cut behind. King Rich's attacker smiled wickedly. He drew his weapon back and tried to thrust forward. With a grunt, King Rich whacked his hand and sent the shank flying across the air. He then kicked him in the nut sack and struck him across the jaw, sending blood flying.

"Arrrrrrrrrrr!" King Rich hollered out, feeling something cold and sharp stab into his back. When he whipped around there was another goon at his back, holding a shank. Another shank was poking up out of his shoulder, trickling blood. King Rich pulled the shank out of his shoulder and threw it down to the ground, causing it to clink on the cool concrete.

"Come on, Pops! I'ma carve yo ass up like a Christmas goose!" The goon that had just stabbed King Rich in the shoulder swore, as he spun his shank around in one hand and withdrew another from his sleeve. The goon rocked a baldhead, but you could tell he had a receding hairline, from the five o'clock shadow growing on his head. There was a trail of four tattoos going down both of his cheeks. Something gleamed in his mouth. When King Rich looked closely, he saw that he had a Gemstar razor inside of his grill.

"Graaaaahhhh!" King Rich threw his head back hollering again, having felt another shank enter his back. He looked to his right and saw a man identical to the one that had just stabbed him. He was definitely the goon's twin. The identical man played with shanks too, just like his counterpart.

A grimacing King Rich tried to pull the blade out of his back but couldn't quite reach it. Before he knew it, he was hollering aloud again, having been stabbed in his calf. He fell down to one knee, looking around at the men that had stabbed him. The three men were actually triplets. Also, surrounding him were the inmates pumping their fists and cheering the goons on to finish King Rich off as he dripped blood on the floor.

The other goons that had come at King Rich were still lying on the floor wincing in pain.

"It's time to pay the piper, old man!" one of the triplets said to King Rich. He and his siblings moved in for the kill.

"Come on then, you sons of bitchez!" King Rich gritted as he finally managed to pull the shank out of his back. Using all of his might, he pushed up from the floor with his cane, standing on his feet on slightly shaking legs. He found his vision growing blurry, and he started to feel weak. Still, he'd be damned if he let those bastards take him out without a fight. "Get down where you're mad at!"

Latrell, who was standing among the other cheering convicts, looked back and forth between King Rich and the goons that wanted his head. He really didn't want to get involved, but he fucked with the old head and he didn't want to see him go out like that.

Fuck it! It's now or never, Latrell thought, making his way through the crowd of inmates swiftly. His eyes were focused on one of the triplets, that was moving ahead of his pack to kill King Rich. Latrell ran out of the crowd, full speed ahead at the goon that was on King Rich's ass. He quickly leaped into the air and came back down hard, kicking that mothafucka dead in the chest. The impact from the blow slammed the lead triplet against a pillar and caused him to drop his shank. Latrell came down and punched another triplet in the jaw, just as he landed on his feet. The punch caused the second triplet to drop his shank. Latrell turned to him and unleashed a flurry of punches to his midsection. He then lifted his ass over his head and threw him at the third triplet. The triplets collided and fell to the floor wincing. Latrell, seeing the first triplet he'd kicked into the pillar going for his shank, ran over to him. He snatched him up by his throat and lifted him off his feet, leaving his legs kicking wildly. The triplet looked down at him with bulging, glassy eyes as he tried to pry his steel-like grip from around his neck.

Latrell stared up at the triplet with arched eyebrows and a scrunched up nose, jaws locked. His eyes bled seriousness and murder. "You and yo punk ass brothers stay the fuck away from the old man, or next time there'll be hell to pay. You hear me, dick sucker? Huh?" Latrell squeezed his neck tighter causing his eyes to bulge further and his veins to pop out of his face.

"Gaaaaagaaaahhh, yes, yes! I, I hear you," the triplet managed to say between gags, tears sliding down his cheeks. His kicking had slowed down tremendously now.

"Good!" Latrell gave the triplet one last squeeze before throwing him to the floor like a rag doll. Latrell then looked up to see his crew beating on the goons that had attacked King Rich. As soon as Latrell had moved in on them niggaz, his squad was right behind him, putting in that work. Seeing that King Rich was on shaky legs, Latrell rushed over to him and grabbed him up under his arm before he could fall. "You okay, OG?"

"Yeah, I'm straight. Thanks," King Rich said, wincing from his wounds.

"Don't mention it."

Latrell helped King Rich over to one of the lunch tables, leaving him leaning up against it. Latrell looked up at the rest of the inmates who were standing around, watching his homeboy kick and stomp the goons that came at King Rich for the last time. Once his crew had finished putting the beats on the goons, they had speckles of blood on their uniforms. Their chests rose up and down as they breathed heavily from combat.

The convicts were still cheering and pumping their fists. They were so loud that they drowned out the stampeding, booted feet of the riot squad, hurriedly heading their way. The riot squad was dressed in black fatigues, protective headgear, shields and black nightsticks. Once the convicts saw the riot squad behind Latrell and his goons, they grabbed their food trays and hurled their food at them. Mashed potatoes, peas, cornbread and meat in brown gravy smacked against the riot squad's headgear, body armor and shields.

Latrell and his goons tried to fight the riot squad, but they ended up getting their asses whipped. They were met with kicks, stomps, whacks upside the head with the nightsticks and sprays of mace that temporarily blinded them.

"Aaaaahhhh!" one of Latrell's goons hollered out.

"Fuuuuck!" another one of his goons cried in pain after being maced.

"Gaaaahhh, my fucking eyes!" a third goon screamed.

They were all sprayed with mace in the face and pummeled with nightsticks to the floor. Afterwards, they were quickly laced with handcuffs and placed on their stomachs.

"Ahhhh, fuck, man! These goddamn cuffs are too fucking tight!" Latrell whipped his locs around and shouted over his shoulder. He was lying on his stomach like the rest of his goons, with the metal bracelets bounding his wrists.

"Oh, yeah? They're too tight? They're too tight? Well, maybe this will help!" one of the riot squad's men, Lewis, smiled devilishly as he blasted Latrell in the eyes with pepper spray. The spray burned like acid, causing Latrell to kick and scream, wincing.

"Aaahhhh, fuck, fuuuck!" Latrell hollered out and squeezed his eyelids shut, trying to shake the burning liquid out of his eyes.

"Piece of shit!" Lewis kicked Latrell in his side and made him squirm in pain.

"Say, bruh, that shit wasn't necessary! Can't you see the man is down with his hands bound behind his—aaaaah!" King Rich howled in pain as Lewis kicked him in the temple. The impact rocked his head and made the world spin. Before King Rich knew it, his eyes rolled to their whites and his head smacked down against the concrete.

"Shut the fuck up, old man!" Lewis spit on King Rich and smiled down at him. He then placed his nightstick to the back of King Rich's skull. If the kingpin wasn't truly knocked unconscious, then he was going to whack him in the back of his head and put his black ass out cold. Seeing that King Rich was unresponsive, Lewis sheathed his nightstick and pulled him up, along with another one of the members of his squad. Through narrowed eyelids, Latrell watched as the kingpin was dragged away. Shortly thereafter, Latrell and the rest of his goons were dragged away.

***

Latrell and his goons were locked up in segregation, while King Rich was hauled down to the infirmary. One week later, he found himself sitting on his bunk playing with the food on his tray. Seeing something at the corner of his eye, he looked and found a dirty brown mouse oozing out of a crack inside the wall. He watched as the filthy creature scurried around on the floor, looking for something to eat. Latrell picked up his slice of stale bread and tossed bread crumbs on the floor, leaving trails to his bunk. A smirk emerged at the corner of his mouth, watching the rodent devour the crumbs that were set out before him.

Latrell crumbled up the rest of his bread and cupped his hand. He brought his hand to the floor and called out to the mouse. The mouse finished off the last of the crumbs on the floor and climbed into Latrell's hand, eating the bread that was in it. Latrell smiled as he watched the rodent eat the bread out of his hand. He caressed its hairy back with his index finger and watched the beady eyed creature nibble on the crumb clutched between his tiny hands.

"You're hungry, man? You're hungry, huh? Eat up! Get cho eat on." Latrell urged him, continuously watching and caressing its back. He could literally see his reflection in the furry animal's black eyes. He was smiling from ear to ear. Latrell was happy to have made a new friend, because it was lonely as fuck being in segregation. Enough time in that mothafucka could drive a man insane.

For the next few weeks Latrell played with the mouse and fed him, watching him grow in size. The mouse wasn't a mouse any more. Nah, he'd grown into a full-blown rat. But Latrell didn't give a fuck. The way he saw it, the little fella was his friend. He was the one that kept him sane while he was locked up.

On his fifty-ninth day in segregation, Latrell stood before the mirror in his cell, looking himself over. His facial hair was wild and bushy, but his locs were tight due to him twisting them up. At six foot two, the Burberry black Latrell was quite the handsome young man. He had a muscular physique and a body loaded with tattoos that you couldn't quite see due to his rich, dark complexion.

Latrell's mother was a thirteen-year-old choir girl that had gotten pregnant by the deacon of the church. Afraid that she'd shame her family if her secret was to ever get out, she had Latrell inside an alley and discarded him inside a trash bin. Not long after, a homeless junkie by the name of Francis came through pushing a shopping cart and rummaging through the garbage looking for something he could possibly sell. He was surprised when he found baby Latrell hidden amongst cardboard and other garbage. He cleaned the little fella up and dressed him up in a sock and an old worn brown shirt.

Francis and Latrell ran cons, scams, stole and robbed niggaz to survive and to feed his habit. At the age of twelve, Latrell lost Francis to AIDS, which he'd gotten from sharing needles. Latrell took care of him until he passed away inside the basement of a condemned house where they were living. From there on, Latrell ran the streets living where he could and doing whatever he had to make it, whether it be robbing or selling drugs.

Thoom, thoom, thoom, thoom!

The iron door rattled from someone rapping on it, then there was a voice. "Chow time, Shepherd!" The corrections officer let it be known before popping open the slot and sliding in Latrell's tray of food. Once he'd gotten it, the C.O. closed and locked the slot back. Latrell sat down on his bunk and got busy with his food, stuffing his mouth. While he was eating, his rat friend, who he'd named Mr. Brown, oozed out of the wall and wandered over to him. Seeing the rodent at his feet, he dropped a piece of his cornbread down on the floor and smiled delightfully. Latrell continued to eat his food as he watched Mr. Brown eat his.

"My man, you must be hungry 'cause you fucking that shit up. What's the matter? Mrs. Brown doesn't cook for you? Yeah, I figured that's what it was. Well, I'ma tell you like an OG once told me, you can get some pussy up outta bitch 'fore you get a hot meal," Latrell commented before continuing to devour his meal. When he looked back over in his tray where he'd picked up his piece of cornbread, he found a kite there. After swallowing his food, he picked up the kite and unfolded it. It was from King Rich. He was presenting him with an opportunity, one that would change his life forever.

Latrell grabbed his pencil and got back at King Rich with the quickness. He sat his kite down in the same place as his carton of milk was and sat the carton back down on it. Latrell then ripped up the kite King Rich had sent him and flushed it down the toilet. Once he finished off his food, he placed it into the slot and pounded on the iron door, calling out the corrections officer's name. A moment later, the slot opened and the corrections officer took his tray and locked the slot back.

***

When Corrections Officer Lewis had gotten off work he was exhausted, but his thirst for pussy overpowered his need for sleep. So, he dipped home, got showered, dressed and headed over to King Henry's Gentlemen's Club on 135th and Crenshaw. He parked his whip in the parking lot across the street from the strip club and made his way over to the stop light, pressing the button so he could cross. As soon as the light turned green, he made his way across the street to the establishment where he was thoroughly patted down by some big burly, baldheaded son of a bitch waiting at the door. Once it was discovered that he wasn't packing concealed weapons, the baldheaded bouncer adjusted his glasses and moved aside so he could walk through. As soon as Lewis crossed the threshold, he was bombarded with loud rap music and the chit chatter of the patrons, as well as the DJ who came over the speakers, announcing the next dancer.

Lewis paid the admission fee at the small window located to his left when he walked inside the strip club. The cashier stamped his hand and he went on about his business, taking in the atmosphere of the gentlemen's club. The patrons were either sitting or drinking as they received a lap dance, talking amongst one another or crowding the stage for the next girl that came out to put on her performance. A tall, high yellow beauty dressed in a hot pink bikini and carrying a platter of drinks made her way past Lewis, but before she could clear his path, he gently grabbed her by the arm. He pulled out a wad of bills, dropping a ten-dollar-bill on her platter and sliding a twenty-dollar-bill between the strap of her bikini bottom.

"I'd like a rum and coke on the rocks, baby. And the twenty is for you." He winked and smiled at her. She flashed him an enchanted smile before thanking him and walking over to the table of men that had ordered the drinks on the platter. Once she'd gone, Lewis found a nice, comfortable spot that wasn't too far away from the stage. He sat down and before he knew it, she brought back his drink. The high yellow chick sat down a napkin first and then his glass of rum right after it. He thanked her and took a sip of his drink, watching the young lady perform on the stage. The goddess he was looking at was Native American, with long silky hair that lay over her shoulders. She had big breasts and a big old ass and she was thick in all of the right places. All she had on was a black thong and thigh-high black leather hooker boots.

She danced provocatively with a brown and black spotted anaconda around her neck as lime green fires exploded at the four corners of the stage.

Froosh, froosh, froosh, froosh!

"Ooous" and "Awwws" erupted from the men on the stage. She walked around to a man standing at the foot of the stage and sex played with him. Taking his Corona, she drank from the bottle and had him lay on his back on the stage. Squatting over his opened mouth, she poured the beer down the crack of her tattooed ass and watched as it filled his mouth. He smiled gracefully and swallowed what she'd given him, just like the trick-ass nigga he was.

Lewis sat where he was in a zone, watching the goddess whose name was exactly that, Goddess. It was like he was under hypnosis. He was completely captivated by her. She'd been keeping her eyes on him the entire time she was performing and working that trick-ass nigga at the foot of the stage. You couldn't tell Lewis that she didn't want him. More importantly, he wanted her and he wasn't leaving King Henry's that night if he didn't have her with him.

One hour later, Lewis was leaving King Henry with Goddess in his passenger seat, unzipping his pants and sucking his dick like it had vanilla cake frosting coming out of it. Rick James's "Super Freak" was pumping from his vehicle's speakers and the windows were down, letting in a cool breeze. The occasional draft had the collar of his shirt flapping up against the side of his face and ruffling his hair and hers. Lewis had his hand lying on top of Goddess's head as she blew him. He kept one eye on the windshield and his other eye on her as she handled her business. The lights from the surrounding streets flashed on and off of him as he kept his other hand on the steering wheel.

At least forty minutes had passed before Lewis was pulling in the driveway of his house. He lay back in the seat and continued to enjoy the mind blowing neck Goddess was giving him. Suddenly, a vein bulged on his temple and his shut eyelids began to twitch as he sneered. He grunted and released his load inside the condom that was covering his dick like a second skin. Goddess came up, popping open the glove box and grabbing the napkins he requested. She gave him a handful to clean himself up and flipped down the sun visor to clean herself up, paying extra close attention to the corners of her mouth where some white shit had accumulated. Once she was done, she flipped the sun visor back up and she and Lewis hopped out of the car, heading up the steps of his home. Goddess put a little extra something-something in her walk as she walked up the steps, because she knew Lewis's thirsty ass was watching her. He smiled delightfully as he massaged his chin and watched that big, fat meaty ass swing from left to right as she hurried up on the porch.

Boy, I'm 'bouta knock the lining outta that pussy! Lewis thought as he pulled out the keys to his home and came up on the porch. He'd just stuck his key inside of the slot in the doorknob when he heard hurried footsteps coming up from behind him and the stripper. When he whipped around, he found a nigga rocking a ski mask and cradling an AA-12 fully automatic shotgun. Lewis and Goddess's eyes nearly popped out of their heads and their mouths hung open when they saw death literally staring them in the face. The gunman turned his AA-12 on Goddess as she turned to run to the opposite end of the porch. He pulled the trigger and fire ignited the end of his barrel and spun her around. The gunman pulled the trigger again and Goddess flew backwards, bumping up against the side of the house. She slid down to the floor, leaving a streak of blood behind on the wall, head tilted aside and eyes cockeyed. Her arms were lying awkwardly at her side and her legs were outstretched in front of her. That bitch was dead!

The gunman, seeing something move in a hurry at the corner of his eye, swung his AA-12 around and pulled the trigger, which pitched Lewis forward. He fell awkwardly to the lawn and started crawling toward his car slowly. The gunman smiled wickedly and displayed his rose gold teeth with the pink diamonds in them. Once he reached Lewis's side, he kicked him over onto his back and looked down at his wincing face as he bled from the corner of his mouth.

"W-what d-did I do?" Lewis croaked in agony.

"You shoulda kept yo hands to yoself!" The gunman pointed his AA-12 at Lewis's head and obliterated it, leaving it looking like Ragu on the grass. He then retreated back to the big black van, which was idling at the curb for him. He hopped into the backseat and the van skirted off in a hurry. Lewis's murder was in retaliation for him putting his mothafucking hands on King Rich back in the penitentiary.

***

On Latrell's sixtieth day in the hole, he gave Mr. Brown what was left of his bread and bid him a farewell. The corrections officer escorted him out of the segregated area and told him that King Rich wanted to see him at the barber shop. Latrell made his way across the prison yard where the other inmates were shooting the breeze, playing basketball, handball or working out. He dapped up the niggaz he knew and mad-dogged the ones he didn't give two fucks about.

Latrell jogged up the steps of the building where the barber shop was located. He made his way down the hall-way, seeing two of his homeboys guarding the door. It was two of the biggest, meanest, blackest sons of bitchez that rolled with his crew, Hugo and Boss Hog.

"I see y'all two niggaz holding it down now." Latrell cracked a grin as he dapped up his homies, showing them that gangsta love they were accustomed to.

"Hell yeah. They let us out of the hole early," Hugo told Latrell. "The old man tried to have the pigs spring you but they wouldn't budge. Said you were one of the main influencers of that brawl, so they hadda make an example outta you."

"Fuck them pigs, man! They can suck my big black dick. They know damn well that shit wasn't right, locking you up like some goddamn dog," Boss Hog said with a scowl. "Hell, they even let those fools we put the beats on out a few days earlier."

"It's all right, baby boy. That lil' bitta time ain't nothing the god couldn't handle. They ain't fade shit. You feel me?" Latrell dapped him up.

"I feel you, big dawg," Boss Hog claimed.

"What the man got y'all out here doing besides watching the door?" Latrell asked as he looked between Hugo and Boss Hog. He spotted King Rich lying back in the barber's chair, while the barber lathered his face with shaving cream. The kingpin looked relaxed as his face was prepared to be shaven, listening to B.B. King's "The Thrill is Gone," which was playing on the small radio sitting on the counter.

"Man told us to pat down every nigga that comes up in here to getta cut. He don't trust a soul and I don't blame 'em either, especially after what had happened that day," Hugo told him. "Gone and holla at him, big dawg. He's been wanted to have a word witchu anyway." He patted him on his shoulder and threw his head toward the door.

"Alright," Latrell agreed.

With that having been said, Boss Hog reached inside of the doorway and knocked on the wall, calling out to King Rich. "Boss-man, Latrell's here to see you."

"Heyyyyy, just the man I've been waiting to see. Let 'em in," King Rich responded, eyelids shut, smile stretched across his face.

Having been given the okay, Hugo and Boss Hog stepped aside to grant Latrell access to the barber shop. Latrell made his way inside the barber shop, looking around. There was six chairs lined up from wall to wall, and King Rich was in the last one. He was currently the only patron at the shop. There was a poster on the wall with different haircuts which were numbered. There were also pictures of famous entertainers on the walls. In the corner of the shop stood the famous red and white striped pole, which was turning slowly.

King Rich peeled open his right eye to see Latrell approaching him. A smirk emerged at the corner of his lips and he stuck out his hand, touching fists with Latrell, who smirked too.

"What's up, OG? I heard you wanted to see me." Latrell said as he stood five feet away from King Rich, arms folded across his chest. A slight scowl accented his brow as King Rich had his undivided attention.

"Yeah, I sent yo goddess that package we discussed."

"Thanks. I appreciate that."

"Don't mention it. You earned it."

Latrell looked around to see that the barber shop was empty, besides his goons that were watching the door. In fact, the only mothafucka inside the shop that didn't hold any affiliation to King Rich was the barber himself.

"Say, how'd you get the man to let chu hold this down like this?"

"Money talks and bullshit walks."

"The power of the dollar."

"Unh huh," King Rich replied with both of his eyelids shut.

As Latrell and King Rich continued conversing, the barber, who was an old man by the name of Bonafide, sharpened his straight-razor on a worn brown leather strap. Bonafide was a baldheaded cat who rocked a beard as thick and as white as Santa Claus's. He was dressed in a white barber's uniform shirt. As Bonafide continued to sharpen the razor, Latrell continued to talk to King Rich, watching him the entire time. He noticed that Bonafide would occasionally glance up at him, looking very suspicious. This brought up Latrell's antennas. He had a feeling something was up, and it made him uneasy. Figuring it was his paranoia, Latrell pushed his worries to the back of his mind, but he continued to watch Bonafide.

"Yeah, man, it's looking like my attorney is going to get them folks to drop that bogus ass murder charge. So, a nigga should be seeing daylight in a minute," King Rich told Latrell.

"That's what's up, G. I'm happy for you."

"Like I was saying to you while you were in the hole, I'ma have 'em take a look at cho case and see what he can do. I'm sure he can make something happen, 'cause he ain't no joke. My man is the D.A.'s worst nightmare, you feel me?"

"I feel you. And I appreciate what chu doing for me also."

"Aye, one hand washes the other both wash the face, if you know what I mean."

"Indeed, I do."

"When you get outta here I want chu to come work for me, full time," King Rich told him, as Bonafide slowly began to shave his face with the straight-razor. "We've already worked out an agreement for you and yours to hold me down behind these walls, but I'd feel much better knowing that you had my back outside of this hell as well. I trust you with my life."

"What about the cat you already got working for you?" Latrell questioned with concern.

"Who? Murda? Shiiiiiit, man, he's not gon' see sunlight for quite some time," he told him straight up. "I need somebody that's gon' shoot first and ask questions last on my behalf. And I cannot see anybody else doing that for me besides you. I want chu to be..."

"A dopeman's bodyguard."

"Exactly," King Rich assured him. "So, what do you say?"

Latrell watched as Bonafide tilted King Rich's head back further in the chair and brought the straight-razor toward his throat, mad-dogging him.

"This is for Montray, mothafucka!"

At that moment, King Rich's eyes widened with fear. Bonafide went to swipe the gleaming blade across the kingpin's throat, when he felt what he thought was iron, slam into his jaw. Blood sprayed out of his mouth and dotted the mirror behind him. Bonafide dropped the straight-razor to the floor. Latrell grabbed him hard and tight by the back of his neck. He then slammed the side of Bonafide's face into the mirror over and over again, causing it to break into a spider's cobweb. Pressing the side of Bonafide's face into the broken mirror, he slid it alongside, crushing more glass into the side of his face.

"Aaaaaaah!" Bonafide hollered out, sounding more like a wounded animal than a man. Latrell yanked Bonafide away from the glass and he stumbled backwards, flipped over the barber's chair. He crashed to the floor and landed hard on his back.

"Yo, what the fuck is up?" Boss Hog called out as he and Hugo came walking inside the barber shop.

Latrell snatched up the straight-razor and began sharpening it on the strap, watching Bonafide as he did so. "Nothing the god can't handle," Latrell answered Boss Hog, but kept his eyes on Bonafide. "Y'all hold this pussy-ass nigga down. Boss-man," he turned to King Rich. "Gone and take a walk, I got this here."

King Rich undid the smock from around his neck and flung it aside. He then made his way outside the barber shop, pulling the door shut behind him. After Hugo locked the door behind him, he joined Boss Hog in holding down Bonafide's arms and legs while that nigga Latrell straddled him. Latrell held the straight-razor in one hand and used the other to pull open Bonafide's shirt, sending buttons flying.

"I'm not gonna kill you, old man. Nah, I'm gonna use you to send a message," an evil-eyed Latrell said as he lifted up Bonafide's undershirt, revealing his nappy, white chest hair. He patted him on his bare chest and opened the straight-razor all of the way up. When Bonafide saw the blade twinkling under the light, his eyes got as big as golf balls and he hollered out for help.

"Helllllllp, hellllp! Somebody, please, help meeeee!" Bonafide hollered and hollered.

"Shut cho bitch ass up!" Latrell smacked the dog shit out of Bonafide, causing his eyes to roll into the back of his head. He was nearly knocked unconscious. Seeing that Bonafide was incapacitated, Latrell pressed the tip of the straight-razor into his right pec, drawing blood. He then pulled the razor downward, spilling more blood. Latrell continued to carve up Bonafide's chest, dotting his own uniform with blood. Even when the old man came to and screamed bloody murder, he went right along carving up his scrawny body.

"From now on, don't nobody fuck with King Rich!" Latrell, with his face dotted with blood, told Bonafide. "The OG is under my protection now. So, fucking with him is fucking with me, and that means death for any parties involved. You dig me?"

"Yeahhhhhhh!" Bonafide hollered out. Right after he did, Boss Hog stuffed his mouth with the smock to muffle his screaming.

Once Latrell finished carving up Bonafide, he wiped the straight-razor off on his pants and stood up, closing the razor up. He looked down at his handiwork, seeing the bleeding message in his victim's chest, Long Live K.R., which stood for King Rich.

CHAPTER THREE

Three years later

King Rich stood before his reflection, half-dressed in his undershirt, slacks and one-thousand-dollar designer shoes. He outstretched his arms as he allowed his youngest son, Baby Boy, to strap on his thin, white Kevlar bulletproof vest. Once Baby Boy finished, he helped him slip on his button down and then his tie, assisting him in tying it. King Rich looked down at his son as he tied the tie, a smirk formed at the corner of his lip.

"I remember when you were a boy and I used to tie your tie every Sunday for church. Now, look at chu, a grown man, tying your old man's tie." King Rich's smirk transformed into a smile, stretching across his face.

Baby Boy Looked up at his old man and smirked as he did his tie. "Yeah, I remember church. Back then, bro and I used to love going to IHOP afterwards. He'd get a big ol' stack of flap jacks and wreak havoc on 'em. Ma used to say he looked like a big, fat swamp possum."

Baby Boy and King Rich busted up laughing, remembering his mother, LaCresha, who'd died of breast cancer three years ago. Diabolic, Baby Boy and King Rich loved her dearly. She was most definitely the glue that held them altogether. Now that she was gone, they were somewhat lost, but still maintaining the best way they could.

"Man, I miss that lady," Baby Boy said seriously.

"I miss her too, son. One day, the four of us will all be back together again."

Knock, knock, knock!

A rapping at the doorway made King Rich and Baby Boy turn around. They found Latrell discontinuing a phone call and stashing his cell phone inside his jacket.

"What's going on, Latrell?" King Rich asked him.

"Yeah, what's up?" Baby Boy inquired as well.

"What's up is, we're gonna be flying out one man short. I just gotta call from Diabolic. He got pulled over and they ran his ass in behind some old warrant. I sent Goldstein down there to bail him out, but I'm sure he's not gonna make this trip," Latrell informed him.

"Well, it's notta big deal. It isn't like we'll be dealing in any hostile situations. I'm just flying out to discuss some business with this cat. We'll be alright," King Rich said.

"You damn straight we'll be alright, especially with me there." Latrell lifted up his shirt and flashed his handgun, winking. King Rich and Baby Boy chuckled.

"Remember, when it comes to Pops…" Baby Boy began.

"Shoot first and ask questions last," Latrell finished what Baby Boy was saying.

"My nigga." Baby Boy smirked and dapped up Latrell.

King Rich slipped on his gold frames and turned from left to right as he looked himself over in the mirror, saying, "Okay. I'm ready now." He adjusted his tie a little and walked toward the door. He faked like he was going to punch Latrell and Latrell jumped back, getting into a boxer's fighting stance. They chuckled and threw playful punches at one another.

"Oh, see there? That one woulda dropped you. The old man still has it." King Rich smiled as he wagged his finger at Latrell. He could have landed an overhand right flush on Latrell's chin, but he pulled his punch at the last minute.

Latrell waved him off smiling and saying, "Mannn, if you don't knock it off, I'll tighten you up."

"Yeah, yeah, yeah, let's get outta here." King Rich laughed and threw his arms around Latrell and Baby Boy's necks as they headed out the bedroom, shooting the shit. King Rich and Baby Boy made their way out of the mansion with Latrell in the middle, hand near his gun in case drama popped off. As they neared the black on black, big-body Navigator, the chauffeur hopped out and opened the back door for them. Baby Boy and his father slid into the backseat. The chauffeur slammed the door of the vehicle, and then he opened the other door for Latrell. Once he was safely inside, the chauffeur slammed the door shut and hopped back inside the truck, pulling off.

Hours after the negotiation in Cochabamba, Bolivia

The Navigator made its way down the road; speeding beside the lines in the center and making them look like blurs. Behind the limousine tinted windows of the big body vehicle, King Rich, Baby Boy and Latrell partook in illegal Cuban cigars to celebrate the deal that King Rich closed hours ago.

"Three hunnit of them thangz at ten a piece? Pops, I don't know how you managed to pull that one off, but I've gotta take my hat off to you. Old man, youz a beast when it comes to coming to the table and negotiating." Baby Boy sucked on the end of his cigar and blew out a cloud of smoke, which mingled with the smoke wafting around his father.

"Well, I hope you took notes, son, 'cause one day this empire is gonna belong to you and yo brother."

"Oh, I was definitely peeping game. I was like a sponge when the whole shit was going down. Mr. and Mrs. Greene didn't raise no fools."

"That's what I'm talking about." King Rich dapped up his youngest son, hugged him and held him against his body, kissing him on top of his head. He was never one to show affection, unless it was to his wife and his two boys. "I love you, son."

"I love you too, Pops."

Latrell sucked on the end of his cigar and blew out a cloud of smoke before speaking. "Well, if you two are done with the mushy stuff, how about we celebrate with a lil' of this drank I got here." He pulled out a bottle of D'ussé VSOP Cognac and handed King Rich and Baby Boy glasses, which already had ice cubes inside of them. He then turned around from where he was sitting and poured the glasses halfway full. Once he finished with their glasses, he poured his own halfway full.

"I'd like to propose a toast to the best father a bum like me could have." Baby Boy held up his glass of alcohol alongside his father and Latrell. "Long live the king!"

"Long live the king!" King Rich and Latrell said together aloud, and then they all clanked their respective glasses together.

***

Vroooom!

A black Ducati ripped up the street, leaving debris in its wake. It dipped in and out of lanes, passing several cars. The driver of the bike was a tall muscular dude, who was wearing a black helmet and leather duster, which flapped in the wind behind him. The beaming sun kissed off the visor of his helmet and cast a rainbow. The driver moved alongside the Navigator, looking back and forth between the bulky vehicle and the street before him. The windows of the truck were limo tinted so he couldn't see who was inside, but he was positive the man he'd come to kill was dwelling somewhere behind the glass. Revving up his engine, the hitta moved ahead to the driver's window. Using his black leather gloved hand, the hitta reached within the recesses of his duster and pulled out an Uzi as black and as cold as his heart. He heard "Long live the king!" coming from the passengers of the bulky vehicle as he pointed his weapon at the Navigator's driver's window. He pulled the trigger of the Uzi, which sounded like a typewriter as it spat rapid fire. The black tinted window shattered and the chauffeur's head slammed down against the horn. As a reflex, the chauffeur's dress-shoed foot mashed the gas pedal and the Navigator sped up. The hitta fired at the front tire of the massive vehicle and the tire exploded, shredding as it sped down the road, coming apart. The Navigator swerved out of control and tumbled down the street, sliding up against a light post.

The hitta pulled up alongside the Navigator and put his Ducati's kickstand down. He then made his way over to the toppled vehicle, pulling a tool from the small of his back that was used to snatch out locks. He leaped upon the Navigator and stabbed the tool into the lock, yanking it out with two tugs and a grunt. Once the lock was out, he plucked it from the end of his tool and tossed it into the street. When he looked up and down the block, he saw bystanders watching him, but looking scared at the same time, filming him with their camera phones. Right then, he pulled his Uzi out and sent some fire their way, causing them to run off in a panic screaming and hollering. He then pulled open the back door of the Navigator and got a chest full of some hot shit.

Blocka, blocka, blocka, blocka, blocka!

The hitta fell to the street. A moment later, Latrell slowly pulled himself out of the Navigator. He was bleeding from the side of his head and clutching a Glock .40. He looked down at the nigga he'd hit up, and then checked his surroundings, seeing people zig zagging back and forth across his line of vision. He ignored them and turned around to the Navigator. Bending downward, he grabbed King Rich's hand and pulled him out of the truck. King Rich, still holding his cane, jumped down into the streets. His eyes got as big as saucers when he saw the hitta rising to his feet and lifting his Uzi up at him. What he didn't know was the hitta had on body armor, so he was impervious to bullets. Seeing his boss about to be splattered, Latrell leaped from the truck and tackled King Rich to the ground, dislocating his shoulder. The men missed the wave of bullets meant to take their lives. The life-threatening bullets left a trail of holes on the hood and rooftop of the Navigator.

"Ahhh, fuck! My ribs!" King Rich grimaced, face balled up, feeling the aftermath of the fall. Latrell looked up and saw the hitta about to open fire again. Swiftly, he rolled across the ground, bringing King Rich along with him, narrowly missing the bullets. The hitta's Uzi jammed up on him. While he was trying to un-jam it, thunder erupted loudly.

Pop, pop, pop, pop, pop, pop, pop!

The hitta dropped the Uzi and fell to the ground. In the blink of an eye, he came back up pulling out a handgun, pointing it at Baby Boy. He was standing on top of the Navigator with his handgun pointed at the hitta, having just unloaded on him. Baby Boy went to fire again, but the hitta was already shooting at him.

Poc, poc, poc, poc, poc!

Baby Boy did a little dance on his feet and fell to the ground, hard.

King Rich shrugged Latrell off of him and scrambled to his feet. "Noooooooo!" King Rich called out with tears in his eyes, having seen his son gunned down in cold blood. He clutched his cane and threw it at the hitta as hard as he could. The cane spun around in circles so fast that it looked like a helicopter propeller, en route toward its intended target. The hitta ducked out of the way of the spinning cane and came up spitting heat!

Poc, poc, poc, poc!

King Rich's eyelids stretched wide open as the bullets slammed into his chest. King Rich looked up at the hitta, accusingly. He then collapsed to the street, wincing.

"Mothafuckaaaa!" Latrell screamed from where he was, veins bulging. He went to point his gun at the hitta, but the mothafucka already had the drop on him, popping off. *Poc!*

Latrell hollered out in agony as a bullet skinned his shoulder and he dropped his Glock, falling back into the street. Grimacing, he looked up and saw the hitta moving in on King Rich to finish him off, handgun extended at him. Right then, he pulled up the leg of his jeans and pulled out a blue steel, snub-nose .38 special from the holster on his ankle. He went to point it at the hitta and he shot it out of his hand. He then shot him in his shoulder and left him howling in pain. With Latrell stunned, the hitta moved in to finish off King Rich. The hitta's shadow eclipsed the older man as he stood over him, pointing his gun at his face, pulling the trigger.

Poc, poc, poc!

With the kill shots having been fired, the hitta tossed the untraceable gun aside. He snatched the gold necklace with the locket on it from around King Rich's neck and stuffed it in his pocket. He then reached within the folds of his duster and pulled out a dead rose, lying it down on King Rich.

Afterwards, the hitta looked over his handiwork, and casually strolled toward his Ducati. After he kicked up the kickstand, he revved up the vehicle and sped off into the sunlight. His motorcycle whined until it disappeared down the street.

"Rich, Rich, Riiiich!" Latrell hollered out to his boss as he crawled toward him, holding his bleeding shoulder, blood seeping between his fingers. He gritted as he moved across the ground. The pain in his shoulder was wreaking havoc on him. By the time Latrell reached King Rich, he knew for sure he was dead. He crossed himself in the sign of the Holy Crucifix and bowed his head, clutching King Rich's cold, dead hand. "Damn, Rich, man! Fuck!" Latrell looked up his boss as tears pooled in his eyes and threatened to spill down his cheeks. Hearing rustling behind him, he searched the ground for his .38 and found it. Picking it up, he pointed it behind him where he heard the noise coming from. He lowered the pistol once he saw Baby Boy coming from behind the Navigator, wincing and pulling open his button down, to reveal a Kevlar bulletproof vest, which had mashed up copper bullets stuck to it. Still wincing, Baby Boy felt underneath his vest, feeling soreness. His mind was taken off his wounds once he laid his eyes on his dead father.

"Pops!" A shocked expression spread across Baby Boy's face seeing his father with a bloody shirt and suit. He ran over to King Rich and slid across the ground like he was trying to reach home base. Baby Boy scooped his dead father's head into his lap and caressed his bloody scalp, staring down into his face, teardrops splashing upon it. Baby Boy's shoulders as well as his entire body shook as he bowed his head. Abruptly, he threw his head back, looking up at the cloudy, graying sky.

"Nooooooo!" Baby Boy screamed aloud, with spit flying from his lips. His pink eyes were wide and flowing with tears. Baby Boy's pained scream grabbed the bystanders' attention. They'd all formed a half-circle around him, Latrell and King Rich. Their brows furrowed and they looked on in awe, watching Baby Boy and Latrell cry their eyes out. By this time, raindrops were falling from the sky pelting everyone's faces and drowning out their tears.

That night

"I'm fucked up, bae. You gotta get me right," Whitney complained out on her grandmother's front porch, pacing back and forth as she smoked a Newport. It was her sixth one within forty-five minutes. She went through cigarettes like hookers went through condoms when she was having withdrawals. "You see how irritable and restless I've been since I haven't had a fix? On top of that, my mothafucking chest hurting."

Whitney was a tall, skinny chick with a head shaped like an ostrich. She had hair she could barely pull back into a ponytail and a bad case of acne. She used to be cute, but crack had aged her considerably. She was far away from the beauty queen that she aspired to be as little girl. But if you were to ask her did she care right now, she'd tell you that she didn't give a fuck. And she wouldn't be lying. All this bitch cared about was getting her next blast.

"What chu want me to do? I'm sick too, and I ain't got no mothafucking money to go cop nothing," an aggravated Tyrell claimed. He was a tall, brown-skinned nigga who was in terrible need of a haircut. He usually rocked his hair in 360-waves, but now his crop was turning into a baby afro. At thirty-one years old, he was once a fairly handsome young man, but smoking all that shit took its toll on his appearance. As of right now, he was dressed in a blue windbreaker jacket, a white T-shirt which he wore underneath it, jeans three sizes too big and a pair of Shaq's that were once white, but now was starting to look light gray, thanks to his continuously wearing them.

Whitney smoked her cigarette down to what was almost considered a butt before dropping it at her feet and mashing it out. She then pulled out another one and lit that bitch up just as fast as she had lit up her last, blowing a cloud of smoke into the air. "Nigga, I don't know what chu gotta do to get me a blast, but do it. You told me if I agreed to be yo girl that you were going to take good care of me. Make sure I have all I want to smoke. Ain't that what chu told me? Huh? Ain't that what chu told me witcho good smooth talking ass?" she asked him as she stepped into his face, making him feel less of the man he was. He bowed his head and scratched his scalp with a bony finger.

"Yeah, I know what I said. I remember," Tyrell told her. "So what do you suggest I do?"

"Them fools over in the Doty Projects be selling crack like it's going out of style. Run up on one of them fools and make 'em come up off you a couple of stones. Shit, I don't know. Look," she took the time to take a pull from off her square and blew out a cloud of smoke before finishing what she had to say. "I got us a place to stay, down in my grandmother's basement, rent free. I made sure we have a pot to piss in and a window to throw it out of. Hell, I even make yo breakfast every morning how you like it, dinner too for that matter. The least yo black ass can do is keep to yo promise of having us something to smoke every now and again. I don't think that's hard. I mean, unless you want someone else taking yo spot." She looked away and took a drag off her Newport, looking out of the corner of her eyes at him to see his reaction. She knew the way to get a man to do what you wanted him to do was to fuck with his ego.

Tyrell's face balled up with anger and he stepped into Whitney's face. "So, what chu tryna say?"

"Humph, I think I'm saying it," she said as she tapped her foot anxiously, dying to have some crack to smoke.

"Nah, see, I need you to make that shit loud and clear."

"Okay, lemme just tell yo slow ass straight up." She looked him straight in his eyes. "if you don't get me high tonight, then you may as well pack up yo shit and go on about cho business. 'Cause I ain't got no holla for a nigga that can't bring nothing to the table."

"Are you fucking for real?" his forehead creased with lines.

"Hell, yes. I don't know what chu think this is, honey."

"After all the times I done hooked yo ass up with some rocks and had you smoking like a goddamn train, this is how you play me?" he asked with both of his hands to his chest, surprised she was talking about kicking him out of her grandmother's house if he didn't deliver tonight.

"Yeah, yeah, yeah, all of those times." She rolled her eyes as she continued to tap her foot. "Well, that's old shit. We're not talking about back then. We're talking about right now. As in right mothafucking now. So, you lemme know how you gon' play this, 'cause I still got time to turn me a trick and get what I need."

Tyrell stood there staring at Whitney like he wanted to punch her head right off of her fucking shoulders. He knew better than to do that though. He'd gone upside her head before and they were fighting in the street like a couple of grown ass men. Old Whitney's uncle owned a gym and he taught her how to fight. She could throw hands just as good as any professional boxer. On top of that, she kept a .44 Magnum revolver down inside of the basement underneath the mattress that he was sure she wouldn't hesitate to use.

"Please, nigga, I know what chu thinking and you know better. I wish a mothafucka would." She looked him up and down like he wasn't shit.

Oh, my God, I hope he doesn't call my bluff. I'm only popping shit like this 'cause I really need 'em to go out there and get me some crack to smoke. Lord knows I wouldn't kick 'em outta the house. I love his skinny black ass too much. He's my boo, Whitney thought.

"You want crack? Fuck it; I'll get chu some crack!" Tyrell ran into the house and returned a couple of minutes later, tucking a black bandana inside of his pocket. He then adjusted the crowbar he'd stuck on his waistline. Without saying a word, he bumped past Whitney and headed off down the block.

CHAPTER FOUR

Shavon stood over the stove whipping up her famous spaghetti sauce, while a pot of noodles boiled in oil and water. At twenty-seven years old, Shavon was a cute caramel-complexioned girl that stood an even five foot six. She wore her hair in blonde individual braids and shaved on the side. She was quick at the mouth and even quicker with her hands. She was a tough girl who'd bring it to any nigga or bitch. Little mama didn't give a mad ass fuck!

"Yooooo, it's hotta than fish grease in here," Shavon complained.

"I know. Niggaz liable to pass out in this bitch," Mank said. Mank was a five foot ten, brown-skinned cat who wore his hair in a close fade. He'd been selling crack since he was old enough to remember. Shavon had tried to get him to try his hand at a trade. But, the call of the streets was too strong for him, so he chose the only life he knew. The life of a hustla.

"Yeah, from a heat stroke," Korey added his two cents. Korey was just as tall as his right-hand man, Mank, except he was light-skinned with deep waves and glasses. He'd lost both of his parents in a car accident when he was sixteen years old and had been shacking up with Shavon, Latrell and Mank ever since. The four of them were like one big happy family.

Mank and Korey sat at the kitchen table cutting up crack and bagging it up, while Shavon went about the task of preparing dinner.

"What chu burning over there, sis?" Mank asked as he wiped his sweaty forehead with the back of his latex gloved hand.

"My famous sauce for this spaghetti," Shavon told him.

"We're having spaghetti tonight, huh?" Mank inquired.
"Yep."

Shavon and Mank's parents were murdered in a robbery gone bad. A meth head tried to stick them up and when he found out they had less than fifteen bucks between them, he murdered them in cold blood and fled the scene, never to be seen again. Shavon and Mank didn't have any family, so they were forced to take it to the streets. Shavon, being eighteen, five years older than Mank at the time, sold her body to provide food and shelter for them. All of that changed once Mank started slinging crack to pitch in. Once he took to the street life, Shavon fell back from prostituting and started stripping at some of the most popular gentlemen's clubs in Southern California.

"Good. Well, I hope it's enough for my man, Korey," he said. Mank and Korey had been homies since the sixth grade. They were more like brothers than best friends. They did everything together. It was rare to see one without the other.

"Boy, you know good and well I made enough for Korey. Hell, how can I forget about 'em, his big head ass lives here." Shavon smiled and smacked Korey upside the head playfully, which caused him to smile. He loved the fact that his ride or die homeboy's family looked at him like he was blood. He always wanted a sense of belonging and they gave it to him.

"Thanks, Shavon," Korey told his sister from another mister.

"No need to say thanks, Korey. Family looks out for another, right?"

"Sho' you right."

"Alright, then. I want y'all to tell me what cha'll think of this sauce here," Shavon said as she scooped a spoon full of her homemade spaghetti sauce into her big wooden spoon, cupping her hand underneath to catch any sauce that might spill. She then carried it over to the youngstaz and allowed both of them to get a taste of it. They smacked their lips and smiled delightfully, loving the taste of her sauce. "What cha'll think?"

"Mmmmm, it's good." Korey nodded his head and wiped the sauce that dripped from his bottom lip with the back of his hand.

Shavon smiled with the approval that she'd gotten from Korey and turned to her brother, Mank, awaiting his verdict. She watched as he continued to smack his lips as if what he tasted was nasty or something. "Well, ol' big head nigga, what chu think?"

"What I think? I think this shit nasty, that's what I think. Yuck!" Mank made an ugly ass face having tasted the spaghetti sauce.

"Hahahahahahaha!" Korey threw his head back laughing and smacking the table top. He knew that that nigga Mank was full of shit. He loved playing with his sister's emotions.

Mank smiled at his sister, letting her know he was just fucking with her.

"Why you play so much, stupid? I'm being dead ass serious right now." Shavon frowned up and playfully punched her baby brother in his arm.

He said, "Ouch," and grabbed the area she'd punched him in.

"It's good, nigga, damn! And yo skinny ass know it's good. Everyone at this table knows you can burn 'cause Mommy taught you," he reminded her.

"Shut up!" She threw a pot holder at his head, which struck him and fell into his lap. "I needa know if I still got it or not. How else am I gonna keep a man?"

"I don't know. But, if you plan on using yo looks then you up Shit's Creek, 'cause..."

Shavon turned the fire off of her sauce and turned around, pointing the wooden spoon at Mank threateningly. "Mank, I swear 'fore God if you don't get off my back, I'ma shove this spoon up yo lil' narrow ass, nigga!" Shavon scowled at him with her lips twisted up. She then swept her individual braids behind her ear and wagged the spoon at him more aggressively than the last time.

"Alright, sis, damn! You can't take a joke?" Mank chuckled as he held his hands up, palms visible.

"Whatever, nigga." She smirked and sat the wooden spoon down. She opened the cabinet and took down the black pepper, season salt, garlic salt and onion powder. She used these ingredients to season the ground beef, which she was going to make into meatballs. The dinner for the night was going to be spaghetti and meatballs, a Caesar salad, garlic bread and chicken wings. It was Latrell's favorite, so little mama knew he was going to be delighted to have it once he'd gotten home.

"Yo, where my nigga Latrell at, sis?" Korey asked as he concentrated on chopping dime-sized rocks off of the hardened, off-white crack patty. Korey had mad love for Latrell because he treated him and Mank like they were his younger brothers.

Shavon stopped and turned around, holding up two fingers on both hands and making air quotation marks. "He's at work," she told him and went back to preparing tonight's meal.

"Oh, okay," Korey responded and he and Mank went about their business of cutting and bagging up crack. Once they'd finished, Mank put most of the rocks inside a freezer bag, while he and Korey stuffed their pockets with what was left.

Mank turned to Shavon, holding up the freezer bag of crack, saying, "Yo, sis, I'ma put this up and me and Korey gon' head out."

Shavon tapped her big spoon on the edge of the pot to rid it of the sauce dripping from it. She then sat it down on the stove top and turned around to her brother and his friend. "You mean to tell me that cha'll asses not gon' eat first before you leave, after I done slaved over this hot ass stove?" she placed her hand on her hip and looked at them with a crinkled brow.

"We tryna hit this block and snatch whatever money is out there. Just put us up a plate, okay?"

"Yeah. I got chu." She turned back around to the stove to tend to the food. Mank returned after putting up the crack and he and Korey bid his sister a farewell before leaving the house.

***

Tyrell walked into Shavon's yard and crept on the side of the house, where a light shined through the window. He peeked inside the window and saw Shavon, Mank, and Korey congregating in the kitchen. The ends of Tyrell's mouth curled up and he licked his lips, rubbing his hands together greedily. He could clearly see that Shavon was making spaghetti sauce and meatballs, while Mank and Korey were cutting the product up and bagging it up.

Yeaaaahh, they gotta 'nough in there to set a nigga straight for a while, boy. I'm glad I brought my shit along with me, Tyrell thought as he pulled the black bandana that was around his neck over the lower half of his face. He then pulled the crowbar from the small of his back and tapped it in the palm of his hand. He moved to the backyard when he saw Mank rise from the kitchen table with a freezer bag of off-white crack cocaine and leave the kitchen. Tyrell found himself at the rear of the house where Mank's bedroom's window was. The light came on inside the bedroom as Mank entered with a bag of crack. He lifted the mattress and stuffed the plastic bag inside the box spring. He approached the bedroom door and looked back at the bed, trying to decide whether or not was something off about the bed, just in case a nigga noticed it and tried to steal his stash out the shit. Figuring that no one would possibly notice, Mank flipped the light switch off and headed out of the bedroom, pulling the door shut behind him.

Once Mank had left the bedroom, Tyrell ran over to the kitchen window and peered inside. He saw Mank and Korey stuffing crack in their pockets and leaving the kitchen, Shavon following behind them. Tyrell crept to the end of the house and peered around the corner to see Mank and Korey leaving the house, with Shavon closing the door behind them, telling them to be careful. Once the youngstaz were gone, Tyrell ran to the back of the house, where Mank's bedroom window was located. He gripped the crowbar with both hands and slammed it into the small opening of the window, flexing it up and down. In doing this, he pried the window open further and further until the opening was wide enough to slip his fingers under. Once he'd gotten the window to this point, he stuck the crowbar into the small of his back again and pushed the window open. Tyrell climbed inside Mank's bedroom and stood upright, smacking the dirt from the windowsill from his latex gloved hands. He then slid the mattress halfway off the box spring and pulled the bag of crack from out of the stash spot, holding it up. The light shining in through the bedroom window illuminated the plastic freezer bag, showing off the off-white crack rocks stored inside. Tyrell smiled victoriously behind his bandana, and as he stashed it inside of his jacket the bedroom door came open. The light switch was flipped on, and Shavon came running inside with a meat cleaver, swinging that bitch wildly. Tyrell's eyes became as big as saucers once he saw Shavon and that big ass meat cleaver with water stains on it.

"Mothafucka, you think you just about to be breaking up in my shit? You gotta 'notha thang coming, bitch! I'm chopping yo mothafucking head, arms and dick off!" Shavon swore with spit flying from her full lips.

Snikt, snikkt, snikkkt!

The meat cleaver sounded off as it whistled through the air coming dangerously close to Tyrell's jugular. When Shavon missed that mothafucka Tyrell's neck, she started swinging at his torso, slicing ribbons out of his shirt.

Snikt, snikkt, snikkkt!

"Hold up, hold up! It's me, it's me!" Tyrell tried to tell her

"I don't give a fuck who you are, yo ass is grass!" Shavon swore as she took more and more swings at him with her meat cleaver which he moved agilely to avoid.

"No! It's me! Tyrell!" Tyrell pulled the bandana down from the lower half of his face and revealed his identity which left Shavon stunned. Her eyes were double their size as she slowly backed away, clutching the meat cleaver and holding her hand to her chest. Her breasts rose up and down as she breathed heavily.

"What the fuck are you doing in here?" she questioned with a crinkled brow. Before he could answer, her eyes darted from the boxspring to him and then back again.

"Nigga, I know you didn't bust up in here to steal my brother's stash witcho smoked out ass!"

"Lemme explain, I—"

"You ain't gots ta explain shit, put it back and put it back now!" She breathed flames as her nostrils flared, pointing the meat cleaver at him.

"I need this, I need this shit!" he pulled out the freezer bag of crack and shook it at her. "If I don't get my fix, I'ma be as sick as a goddamn dog!"

"That's yo problem; I don't give a fuck no more! I tried to get chu help, but chu didn't want it so I washed my hands with the situation!"

"Like I told you then, I'll get help when I'm good and ready. And right now I'm not quite ready," Tyrell told her straight up as he stashed the bag back inside his jacket. "Look, I've gotta breeze, I'll replace this shit later." He moved to head for the door but Shavon slid into his path, blocking it.

"You not leaving my house with my baby brother's shit, nigga! You got me totally fucked up! Put that shit back!" She scowled at him.

"No can do, now move!" he scowled at back her.

"So help me, Tyrell, if you don't put back what doesn't belong to you, nigga, I'ma cut cho skinny, black poor ass in half," she threatened and gritted, veins bulging on her forehead.

"The only way you're getting this bag back is over my dead body!" Tyrell swore to her, balling his fists at his sides.

"So be it!" Shavon roared and took a few swipes at Tyrell with the meat cleaver. Tyrell avoided the blade masterfully and countered back.

He kicked Shavon so hard in her stomach she made an "Ooof," and doubled over, holding her torso, dropping the meat cleaver to the floor. Before she knew it, Tyrell was backhand slapping her with all of his crackhead strength, knocking her to the floor. Shavon slammed down on the carpeted floor face first. Tyrell followed up by stomping her head and then kicking her in her side, which caused her eyes to bug and her to gasp. The vicious blow had knocked the wind out of her, and left her gasping for air.

"I didn't wanna do that, but chu brought that upon yo self! I told you to just lemme gon' 'bout my business with this lil' trap here, but chu just wouldn't lemme go. Now, look at cha, lying on the floor in a world of hurt." With that having been said, Tyrell made his way for the door, walking past a portrait on the nightstand beside the flat screen television set. Tyrell stopped and took a gander at the portrait. It was of him, Shavon, a younger Mank, and their late son, JaQuawn. He picked up the portrait and stared at it a second before putting it back where he'd picked it up from. "I'm sorry but your momma left me no choice, son." He continued out the door with Shavon hurling insults at his back.

"Tyrell, its ten o'clock at night and you finna teach 'em how to ride a bike? Maybe you should just take 'em out tomorrow at the park" Shavon suggested as she stood in the doorway of the house, watching Tyrell walk out the yard behind their five-year-old son, JaQuawn, who was on his bicycle. The little dark-skinned, loc-haired boy looked so excited and cute on his bicycle. He was wearing his protective Superman helmet, as well as his elbow and kneepads. Little man couldn't wait to show his father how well he could ride his bike.

"Lil' man wants to show me what he's got tonight. It's okay, lady bug, we'll come right back in once he shows me he can ride like I taught 'em to." Tyrell opened the gate to

the front yard and stepped aside so JaQuawn could walk his bike out. Once the boy was out and had mounted his bicycle, Tyrell smiled like the proud father he was, watching his boy ride off down the sidewalk.

"See, Daddy? I'm doing it, I'm doing it!" JaQuawn said over and over again as he pedaled off hastily.

"I see you, son. I'm so proud of you, man. This is cause for a celebration. How's about Disney Land?" He smiled at his baby boy's back as he watched him pedal away expertly.

"Cool! I'm going to Disney Land! Whoohoo!" JaQuawn hollered out excitedly as his mother, Shavon, looked off from the front porch. She was smiling with her arms folded across her breasts and a dish rag over her shoulder. She was doing the dishes when Tyrell decided to let JaQuawn show him he knew how to ride his bike.

Right then, something at the corner of Tyrell's eye caught his attention and he looked over his shoulder. From the shadows a dark figure in a hood emerged. All he could see was the lower half of the man's face and the big rose gold Cuban link chain he was wearing, which held the medallion of a money bag with a dollar sign on it. Pink diamonds flooded the Cuban link chain and its piece. The man smiled satanically as he licked his diamond and rose gold teeth, coming from underneath his hoodie with the barrel of the world's longest revolver. The illumination coming from the street light kissed off of the barrel, just before the man extended it to take a shot.

Tyrell's eyes grew as big as bowling balls and his mouth dropped open. He looked down the sidewalk and saw an unaware JaQuawn pedaling up the block. At this moment, he shouted to Shavon in slow motion and a weird ass voice.

"Get JaQuawn, Shavon! Get the baby!" he said as the man had taken aim at him, and pulled the trigger of his pistol.

The chamber twisted and sparks flew from the mouth of it. Tyrell winced and gritted as a hot one ripped through his shoulder and propelled him backwards into the gate behind him. He fell up against the gate, but came up blasting with a cannon of his own, getting busy in the streets with the shooter that had peeled himself from out of the darkness to claim his life.

Boom, boom!

Bloc, bloc, bloc, bloc!

"Bitch ass nigga, got the balls to get at me while I'm at my crib? That's yo ass, homeboy!" Tyrell swore as he and the gunman moved counterclockwise behind the shielding of parked vehicles, taking shots at one another. While this was going on, a panicked Shavon was running down the steps of the house in a hurry to get to JaQuawn before he could be shot down.

Boom, boom, boom!

Bloc, bloc, bloc!

The back window of a parked Dodge Intrepid shattered and the gunman hollered out, doubling over as he cringed. He'd been shot in the cheek. The gunman touched his bleeding jaw and his fingertips came away bloody. He then leaned over the hood of the Dodge Intrepid, squeezing the trigger of his revolver vengefully. After he got off the last of his bullets, he took off running down the sidewalk, warm, smoking Magnum in hand.

Bloc, bloc!

Tyrell took off running after the gunman firing shot after shot. Once the gunman was swallowed up by the night, Tyrell slowed his running to a jog and stopped in the middle of the street. He looked around in the darkness for the gunman from where he stood, but he couldn't find him. As his adrenaline began to slow down from its intense pumping

Tyrell touched his shoulder and his hand came away bloody. At that moment, he heard Shavon's horrified screams and looked over his shoulder. He found Shavon down on her knees with JaQuawn in her arms. The boy had a bleeding hole in his chest and he was wheezing for air, pupils moving around aimlessly. A couple of feet away was JaQuawn's bicycle, which was toppled over with droplets of blood trailing from it.

"No, no, no, no, no, God, help me! God, please help me! Not my boy! Not my sweet lil' baby boy!" Shavon cried out, with big teardrops dripping from the brims of her eyes and splashing on JaQuawn's face. Green snot bubbles formed out of her right nostril and oozed down over her top lip, she was crying so hard. She looked up into the sky and talked to the Almighty Lord, saying, "Please, Lord, don't take 'em, don't take 'em! My baby ain't never done nothing to nobody! He's a good boy! He's a sweet good boy! Have mercy on him, Father, and take me! Take meeeeeeee!" When she looked down at her son's innocent face, his pupils dilated and he took his last breath, muscles relaxing, body going still. At that moment, Shavon knew that her precious baby boy was gone. Right then, she bowed her head and cried out hardily.

As the police car sirens wailed in the distance, Tyrell got down on his knees beside Shavon. He swept his baby boy's eyelids closed with the sway of his hand and kissed him tenderly on his forehead. Tyrell then kissed Shavon on the temple and bowed his head, crying long and hard, holding on to the last precious moments he had with family.

Tyrell was the neighborhood dope man and he was rising in status, power, dirty money and street fame. All of this drew the attention of King Rich's organization who met him with a proposition, either buy his drugs from them or leave the game alone—period. When Tyrell told them to kiss his rich black ass, they sent one of their top hittas at him. Tonight was the result of the botched execution.

After the devastating loss of his only child, Tyrell turned to the drug that he sold to cope, crack cocaine. It wasn't long before he was a full-fledged crackhead, doing any and everything that he could to support his habit, once he spent up his small fortune from selling the narcotic. Shavon did try to help him get clean, but he wasn't having it. So she left him, to deal with his addiction and the tragedy that changed his life forever.

"That's gon' be the last time you put cho hands on me, mothafucka! The last goddamn time!" Shavon scrambled to her feet and ran down the hallway, dipping off inside of her bedroom. She flipped on the light switch and ran over to the closet, swinging open the door. She pulled the drawstring inside the closet and restored light inside the space. She felt around on the top shelf of the closet until she came upon a two-tone, black plastic and metal Glock .40. She grabbed that bitch and cocked it, putting one in the head. She came back down with the gun and stared at it. Knowing if she went after Tyrell with it she'd definitely kill him, and she wasn't sure if she was ready to murder him when she still had love for him.

Shavon looked to her right and saw a dozen golf clubs inside a tan and brown bag in the corner of the closet. Her mind bounced back and forth from the golf bag to the blower in her hand. She placed the blower back at the top of the closet and turned to the golf bag, pulling one of the golf clubs from out of it. She stepped out of the closet with the golf club and practiced swinging it expertly. The golf club swooshed as it swung through the air, back and forth. Once she figured she could do some damage with the golf club,

Shavon ran out of the room and down the hallway. She found Tyrell's back as he was about to open the front door.

"Fuck you think you're going, bitch?" Shavon roared, with spit flying from her lips again, swinging the golf club. Tyrell had just turned around and ducked, but the side of his head ended up getting clipped by the club. Tyrell grabbed the side of his head and staggered across the living room with Shavon striking his ass with the golf club again.

"Ah, ahh, ahhh, what the fuck, man?" Tyrell hollered out as he ran around the living room with Shavon striking him repeatedly with the golf club. Shavon cocked the golf club back over her head and swung it downward with all of her might. Tyrell caught the golf club in his hand and kicked her in the stomach, sending her flying across the room. She knocked over a lamp, which fell to the floor and broke. She landed on the floor right beside it, wincing. "Bitch, what the fuck is wrong witchu, hitting me upside my mothafucking head with this mothafucking golf club?" he threw the golf club across the living room. "I'ma stick my mothafucking foot in yo ass!"

Tyrell grabbed the back of Shavon's shirt and slung her up against the wall, causing her to bump her head up against it. Tyrell swooped in and wrapped his hands around her neck, choking the dog shit out of her. He lifted her off her feet, causing one of her slippers to fall off her feet. His pupils were two burning orbs as he stared into her eyes and bit down on his bottom lip. "I'll kill you, I'll fucking kill you for coming at me like that! Coming at me like I'm some kind of bitch ass nigga, hoe! You know my background, you know a nigga used to be the king of these mothafucking streets!" he told her as he shook her and shook her, choking her harder and harder. Veins formed all over Shavon's forehead and neck and her eyes turned glassy and red webbed. Shavon clawed and clawed at his hands, breaking one of her hot pink painted nails in the process. She was hoping to get him to let her go, but her efforts were useless. So, she started clawing at his face. Tyrell whipped his head from left to right to avoid the assault. "Ahhhhh, you fucking whore!" Shavon slid further down the wall as Tyrell's grip on her neck weakened. This leveled her foot at his crotch. She took advantage of the situation and kicked him as hard as she could in his balls. Tyrell dropped Shavon to the floor and grabbed his privates, falling to the floor beside her. He bawled on the carpeted floor wincing and crying his eyes out from the agonizing pain.

"Huff, puff, huff, puff, huff, puff!" Shavon lay on her back struggling to breathe and massaging her sore neck. The pain around her throat had lessoned but she was still light-headed. She looked over at Tyrell, seeing blurred doubles of him. She was too weak to fight him. All she could do was watch as he struggled up on his feet and limped out of the house, holding himself.

Shavon lay on the floor breathing heavily and looking around. She shut her eyelids briefly, peeling them back open when she heard her cell phone ringing. Slowly, she got to her feet and staggered down the hallway to her bedroom where she discovered her cellular on the nightstand. Its screen lit up as it rang and vibrated. She picked it up. It was her boo, Latrell. "Oh shit!" Shavon said as soon as she saw her man's name. She cleared her throat with her fist to her mouth and took the time to gather herself before answering the call. "Heyyyyyyy, baby, how're you? What? Oh, my God! Latrell, what happened? What hospital are you at? Okay, I'll be there in a sec. Okay. I love you. Bye."

Shavon disconnected the call and grabbed her purse, dropping it inside. She then grabbed her makeup bag and dipped off to the bathroom where she applied makeup to her forming blackish blue eye and the hand prints around her neck. She wasn't about to tell Latrell or Mank that Tyrell broke inside their house and stole his stash, because she knew they'd most likely kill him. Well, that nigga Latrell definitely would smoke him for putting his mothafucking hands on her. You see, Latrell was madly in love with Shavon and didn't play when it came to her. Nah, he'd have a nigga getting outlined in chalk real quick.

***

Whitney set on the porch of her grandmother's house smoking a withering Newport and tapping her foot impatiently. She'd been waiting on her man, Tyrell, to return for the past two hours. He said he was going to cop them some crack so they'd be set right for the next couple of days. She didn't believe him because he was just as broke as her, but she knew Tyrell had a habit of completing any task he put his mind to. This was what had drawn her to him in the first place. He was an ambitious bastard that wouldn't take no for an answer, hell, that was how he had bagged her way back in high school. They were high school sweethearts. She was a cheerleader and he was the quarterback. They ended up going on to be the prom's king and queen. But, they broke up shortly after graduation because she found out he had other chicks on the side. Fate was a mothafucka though because they both wound up getting strung out on crack and finding their way back to one another. And here they were, the self-proclaimed king and queen of the mothafucking ghetto—yeah right.

"Goddamn, where the fuck is this nigga at? I needa get right." Whitney took a couple of more puffs of her Newport and dropped it at her feet, mashing it out under her flip flop. When she looked back up and saw Tyrell coming up the block, she smiled from ear to ear, showcasing her missing teeth. She stood upright as Tyrell entered the yard smiling at her. "Did you get it?"

"What's my name?" Tyrell smiled.

"Did you get it?" she asked again.

"What's my mothafucking name?" He looked around to make sure there wasn't anybody eyeballing him before he pulled out his freezer bag of crack.

"Tyrellll!" Whitney screamed with excitement and leaped into Tyrell's arms, wrapping her arms and legs around him. He spun her around and they kissed long and hard, smiling.

Tyrell set Whitney down and she grabbed him by his hand, leading him inside the house where they journeyed down in the basement and smoked crack together.

CHAPTER FIVE

Latrell lay up in bed deep in his thoughts as the television played the news of the event that had taken place earlier that day. Baby Boy was also in the room, standing before the enormous window, watching pigeons attack a piece of bread. When Latrell looked over at him, all he could see was his back and the reflection of his face, which was shown through the slightly dirty window. Baby Boy's eyes were pink and glassy and there were teardrops falling from the brims of his eyes. His face was fixed with a scowl and his fists were balled at his sides. The man had just lost his father and Latrell wasn't sure what he could say to him that would ease his pain, but he knew within his heart that he had to say something. He owed it to him, seeing as how he was the one who was assigned to protect King Rich's life and he'd failed.

"Look, I'm not good with words. In fact, I'm horrible when it comes to expressing myself, but I've gotta tell you that I'm sorry for what happened out there. I mean, I'm really, really sorry, Baby Boy. I tried my best to hold yo father down, but in the end I failed not only you, but him," Latrell's eyes welled up with tears, but he blinked them back. He was feeling emotional as fuck, but held back the pain that was threatening to spill from his heart. Homie had loved King Rich like a father, and King Rich had loved him like a son. The kingpin's death had hurt him just as much as it had hurt Baby Boy. Shit broke his heart, and it was engraved in his mind to find the son of a bitch that had downed him and took his life. No matter what!

Baby Boy bowed his head and shut his eyelids. As soon as he did, hot tears streaked down his cheeks and dripped off his chin, splashing on the floor. He took the time to wipe his dripping eyes with the back of his fist and looked back up, focusing out of the window as he talked to Latrell. "Shit's fucked up, fam. Shit's real fucked up. I keep replaying everything over and over again inside my mind, thinking of what I coulda done to stop this shit from happening so pops could still be alive." Baby Boy took a deep breath and turned around to Latrell, grief sliding down his face. "All this shit ain't on you, my nigga. I shoulda got the truck bulletproofed like Pops had been asking me to. Had I done that, maybe he'd still be alive. I also shoulda hired extra security too."

"Fuck alla that! This shit is his fault!" a voice rang out from the door of the hospital room. When Baby Boy and Latrell looked at the door, a tall, lanky, caramel-skinned nigga with big lips and a baldhead strolled inside the room. He had a money bag with a dollar sign tattooed beside his right eye. He also had a mouth full of pink diamond teeth and a Cuban link chain that hung down to a money bag medallion with a dollar sign on it. The chain was rose gold and had pink diamonds in it, and so did the money bag medallion. This was Diabolic, King Rich's oldest son. He was the enforcer of the organization. As of right now, he was wearing a camouflage L.A. fitted cap and matching hoodie.

Latrell mad-dogged Diabolic and balled his fists up, veins bulging in them.

"Fuck you looking at me like that for, nigga? I ain't telling no lies! You were hired to protect my father, and you didn't! He's dead! And it's yo mothafucking fault! His death rests on yo shoulders!" Diabolic spat and jabbed at the air with his finger, spit flying from off of his lips. He went to move toward Latrell while he was in bed, but Baby Boy slid into his path, blocking his path.

"Stop that shit, man! We're not pointing fingers, and we're not putting the blame on anybody here! You got that?" Baby Boy looked back and forth between Latrell and

Diabolic, scowl fixed on his face. He walked away from Diabolic, leaving him and Latrell mad-dogging one another as he looked out of the enormous window again. "I have an idea of who got at Pops." When he said this, Diabolic and Latrell broke their mad-dog stares and looked at him.

"Who?" Latrell and Diabolic asked in unison.

"Montray." Baby Boy tossed the name out there.

"Montray? That doesn't make any sense. That beef has been dead for years," Diabolic reminded him.

"Nah. The streets have been talking and Montray has been planning an attack for quite some time now. I ignored them, 'cause like you, I figured that beef they had was put to bed," Baby Boy said. "But, the death of Pops proves otherwise."

"Raaaaaaah!" Diabolic flipped over the rolling table that had Latrell's dinner on it, spilling the food on top of it. "Fuck!" he swung on the air a few times in a rage. He swung back around to Baby Boy's nostrils flaring and chest rising and falling, breathing heavily. He was as hot as fish grease, having found out that Montray had had his father murdered. He had told his father to let him smash dude when he had the chance, but he decided to let him slide. Now, he was feeling like he was partially to blame for his old man's death because in his mind if he would have popped Montray then King Rich would still be alive.

"Now, that we know whose behind Rich's death, what do we do now?" Latrell asked Baby Boy.

Baby Boy frowned up and bit down on his bottom lip, slamming his fist into his palm for emphasis, saying, "We smash his ass."

"Whenever you ready to make that move, you be sure to lemme know, 'cause I'm all in," Latrell assured Baby Boy.

"That's love." Baby Boy slapped hands with Latrell and embraced him, patting him on the back. He then stood upright and looked to Diabolic, giving him a look like, *come show the homie love, nigga.* With that gesture, Diabolic took a deep breath and embraced Latrell, patting him on his back. Diabolic then rolled his eyes as if he was annoyed. Although he partially blamed himself for what had happened to his father, he still felt like most of the blame was to be placed on Latrell, since he'd been hired to be his bodyguard.

"When it's time to make that move, I'll be in touch." Baby Boy patted Latrell's leg and headed out the room alongside Diabolic. As soon as they disappeared through the door, a couple of minutes later, Shavon came hurrying in over the threshold and over to Latrell's bedside. She hugged him and kissed him all over his face, wiping her moist eyes once she pulled away from him.

"Bae, I was so, so scared when I got the call. Are you okay?" Shavon looked over him carefully, seeing the red dot on his bandaged arm.

"Yeah, I'm okay, but King Rich is dead." He looked at her with sorrowful eyes, looking like he was on the verge of tears again. This made Shavon tear up too. She knew just how close King Rich and her boo were, so she knew his heart had to be aching terribly.

***

Baby Boy and Diabolic walked in the elevator. Diabolic pressed the button for the lobby and the double doors shut. Big teardrops fell from Baby Boy's eyes as he bowed his head and balled his fists at his sides. His right eyelid and the corner of his top lip twitched. Suddenly, he hauled off and punched the wall, creating a "dong" sound as his fist deflected off the surface.

"Damn, Pop, damn! How the fuck we let this fool catch us slipping like this? We were supposed to have been on point, on our toes and ready for this shit, man. Goddamn!" Baby Boy punched the wall again and it created the same noise. Diabolic looked over his shoulder at his younger brother and felt his pain. He pressed the red emergency stop button. He then walked over to him and gave him a brotherly hug. Diabolic was teary-eyed, but tears seemed to be constantly flowing down Baby Boy's cheeks.

"It's okay, bro. We gon' get this nigga that murked Pops. I swear to God, homie's day is coming. But, in the meantime and in between time, we gotta keep the empire going. That's the way Pops would have wanted it. You helm the throne while I play guard, keeping these bitchez and these bitch ass niggaz in check, you feel me?" Baby Boy nodded and sniffled, wiping his dripping eyes with his curled finger after breaking his brother's embrace. Diabolic turned around and pressed the emergency stop button again, which made the elevator continue on its way down. "When the next shipment of this new shit hitting that Pops just negotiated?"

"The drop coming in two days."

"Good."

"I was thinking about getting Pops cremated and getting us some mini gold urns with his ashes to rock around our necks. What chu think?"

Diabolic nodded and said, "Yeah, I'm all for that idea."

"Cool. 'Cause tomorrow I'ma roll out to make the arrangements to make it happened. I was thinking that maybe you'd wanna roll with me."

"What time?"

"Eight sharp."

"We're on then." Diabolic dapped him up. He then threw his arm around his shoulders and walked out of the elevator with him, joking around.

***

Having nearly lost Latrell had Shavon feeling sexual and extremely horny. She asked him was he trying to get busy and he was with it. An excited Shavon walked over to the door and locked it. She then walked over to Latrell, pulling her skirt all the way up so her panties were visible. As she approached his bed, she could see the tall tent his rock-hard dick had made underneath the sheets. She peeled the cover back and lifted up his hospital gown, revealing his erect manhood which was riddled with veins and rooted from a nest of nappy hair. The sight of it made her that much wetter between her legs, and she felt that flap of flesh between her pussy lips pulsating, like it had its own heartbeat.

Shavon pumped Latrell's dick gently, feeling it grow harder and harder in her firm hand. Before she knew it, Latrell's shit was brick hard and clear fluid was running out of his pee-hole. On top of that, his dick was so hard and pulsating, the veins running up and down through it looked like they were about to rupture at any minute. Seeing her man so ripe and ready got Shavon going for real, for real. She licked her full lips excitedly as she brought her mouth to his manhood, looking up at him as she took him inside her salivating mouth. Latrell moaned like a straight-up bitch, feeling his woman's inviting mouth wrapped around his pole, going up and down him, spilling some of her hot juices on him.

"Mmmmmmmmm!" Shavon moaned and groaned as she brought her head up and down her man's full potential, eyelids narrowed into slits, hand jerking him off as she sucked him.

"Sssssss! Ooooooh, shit, man. Goddamn! You tryna suck the soul outta nigga, boo. Fuck!" Latrell stated the obvious with his eyelids closed, biting down on his bottom lip. He laid his hand down on Shavon's head and started humping her mouth slowly at first and then a little faster, causing her to gag, veins bulging at her temples and neck. She continued to whip her mythical head game on him, driving him crazy and causing his big toes to point up at the ceiling. He grabbed hold of her individual braids and looked down at her as she looked up at him, sucking him feverishly, making nearly all of him disappear inside her mouth. "Ahhh, fuck, I'ma 'bouta cum, babe! I'ma 'bouta cum!"

There was a loud suction sound as Shavon popped Latrell's dick out of her mouth, saying, "No, the fuck you not! You 'bouta get up between these walls 'fore you do anything else!" she assured him as her fist pumped his hot, throbbing dick. She stared him dead in his eyes as she jacked his ass too, more and more of that see-through fluid ran out of his pee-hole. That mothafucka was hot and horny and it was written all over his face and body. He wanted her. He needed her. He had to have her, in the worse kind of way.

As soon as Shavon climbed into the bed and straddled Latrell, he grabbed her by her waist. She moved her panties aside and exposed her fat peach. She then took hold of his thumping dick and lined him up with her warm hole, easing herself down onto him, feeling him fill up her void, stretching her open wider than she already was. A blissful expression crossed her face and she threw her head back as she felt her man inside of her slippery womb.

Shavon moved her stretch-marked ass up and down Latrell's dick. Her pussy slowly oozed with a white lather that slid down his endowment, slicking it wet. She dug her manicured nails into his chest and threw her head back, biting on her bottom lip, moving her hips like a cobra snake coming out of a wicker basket. Shavon moaned and groaned the faster she moved and so did Latrell. He was enjoying how warm and tight her twat was, allowing his strong hands to sink into her meaty buttocks. He threw his head back into the pillow, squeezing his eyelids shut and biting down on his inner jaw. He felt like he was going to explode inside of her and he didn't know how long he was going to be able to fight off the feeling.

"I'ma 'bouta cum, ma! I'ma 'bouta cum right now!" Latrell warned her as he felt himself about to erupt.

"Not yet, baby. I'm almost there, I'm almost there! Ooooou!" Shavon licked her lips and bit down on her bottom one, continuing to move her body like a snake, going faster and faster, making her man's dick hit her G-spot over and over again, enjoying every minute of it. "Yes, yes, right there, baby! Right there, I'm 'bouta cum! I'm 'bouta fucking cum!" she looked down at him with wide opened eyes and mouth hanging open. A vein at her temple was jumping, looking like it was about to burst. She felt herself about to explode and drench him with her pussy's natural nectar.

"Me too!" Latrell's eyelids fluttered white and he clenched his jaws hard as fuck.

"Oh, my fucking Godddddddddd!" Shavon hollered out and trembled all over as her love came down, drenching her lover below her. Right after, Latrell pulled her down against him and pulled out of her, resting his dick against her left buttock. He jacked himself off and shot string after string of white, warm cum out on her, rubbing it on her meaty behind. He then exhaled and his body went rigid as he breathed heavily. She kissed him all over his face and then on his mouth. They made out for a minute before they heard a knock at the door. Hastily, Shavon hopped off of him and used a few napkins that were at his bedside to wipe herself clean. She balled up the napkins and threw them inside the waste basket before grabbing her purse. She took out a bottle of Chanel No5 perfume and sprayed the air to mask the smell of sex that consumed the air. Afterwards, she straightened out her clothing and took a deep breath before unlocking the door.

An Asian nurse walked in wearing glasses, her hair pinned up in a bun and a stethoscope around her neck. Her hands were filled with documents which she presented Latrell with after saying "Hi," to Shavon. "Okay, Mr. Shepherd, this is your discharge paperwork. And this is your prescription for your Tramadol, you take it as prescribed. It tells you your dosage right here." She pointed it out to him on the paperwork.

"Okay. I see it."

"Alright. Well, I'ma give you time to get dressed while I get your wheelchair to roll you outside to your car."

"Okay. And thanks you so much, Beverly."

"You're welcome, no problem," she told him with a smile and walked out of the room.

Shavon walked over to Latrell and wrapped her arms around him, staring him in the eyes adoringly as he held on to her waist. "Sooooo, are you ready to get outta here, Mr. Shepherd?" she smiled at him.

"Only if you're coming with me, Mrs. Powell." Latrell smiled back at her and they kissed romantically. When she pulled back, he noticed something off about her face. "Hmmmm," he said as he tilted his head to the side and looked at her curiously, narrowing his eyelids.

"What? What's wrong?" Shavon frowned up, wondering what had caught his attention.

"What happened to your face?" He poked the slight swelling below her right eye.

"Ouch!" she jumped and touched her face gently.

"Were you fighting someone earlier tonight?" he questioned with concern, as he followed her over to the mirror residing over the sink. She looked over her reflection as he stood behind her studying her face.

"No, I was bitten by a spider," she lied.

"A spider? Was it inside the house?"

"Yeah, I was making spaghetti and I went to grab something from the pantry and I got bit. No need to worry though, I'll be fine." She turned around to him and threw her arms around his neck once again, looking up at him smiling.

"You sure? You don't wanna get checked out while we're here at the hospital?"

"Nah, baby, it's just a lil' bite, it'll heal eventually. Now gemme some lip, handsome." She leaned in for a kiss, and they locked lips, kissing slowly and passionately.

The next morning

Latrell's nostrils flared as the smell of bacon wafted its way into his nose. His nostrils twitched and his eyelids fluttered as he began to stir awake. His eyelids peeled open and he sat up in bed, rubbing away the crust that had formed in the crevasses of his eyes while he slept. He looked to the side of the bed where Shavon had slept and saw she was gone. Latrell slipped on his wife beater and a pair of basketball shorts he'd retrieved from out of the top nightstand drawer. He stepped inside the bathroom where he washed his face and brushed his teeth, taking care of his hygiene. Once he was done, Latrell carried his muscular body into the kitchen where the scent of a scrumptious breakfast had brought him. When he entered the kitchen, Shavon was standing at the kitchen counter raking eggs into a plate of food. Mank and Korey were already grubbing up. Their plates were loaded with eggs, bacon, potatoes, and cinnamon toast.

Shavon picked up the plate of food and turned around. Seeing her nigga brought a smile to her face. "Good morning, handsome."

"Good morning, beautiful." Latrell pecked Shavon on the lips. She sat his plate down before him and he smacked her on the ass playfully. She then walked over to the side of the table she was going to sit and sat down.

Latrell looked at Mank and Korey, dapping them up. "What's up, my young niggaz?"

"What up, G?" Korey greeted him.

"What's good, bro, how're you feeling?" Mank asked.

"I'm doing okay. Wounds still aching, but I'ma pop a few killaz once I eat."

"Hold up. Now, I know you two trifling ass Negros aren't eating before we say grace." Shavon frowned up at Mank and Korey, snatching their forks out of their hands and dropping them back down into their individual plates.

"Aw, come on now, sis. I'm starving like a hostage," Mank complained.

"Man, that's what I'm saying," Korey said. He was hungrier than a mothafucka too.

"You two niggaz can bitch all you want to, but we're not eating until we say grace. Now, gemme ya hands." Shavon said and extended her hands. Everyone at the table held hands and Shavon started saying grace to bless the food before they all ate. Once she had finished, everyone began eating their food and talking.

"So, when is your boss's funeral?" Korey inquired as he stuffed his face.

"He's not having one. His son is going to cremate 'em."

"Cremate 'em, huh? The day I die I want my ashes spread throughout the hood."

"Cremated? Fuck that! Bury me a G," Mank said before taking a bite of bacon.

"I heard that," Korey said before wiping his mouth. He then tapped Mank. "Yo, it's time we hit the streets and give the fiends their prescriptions."

"Right." Mank finished the strip of bacon and downed the last of his orange juice quickly. He then wiped his mouth off and rose from the table. "Come on," he said to Korey before they both dapped up Latrell and pecked his sister goodbye.

***

Korey and Mank kicked it on the block, shooting the shit and serving the occasional crackhead that would come through every now and then. Mank spit off to the side. The nasty glob that flew from his lips splattered on the edge of the curb. He screwed the cap off his Yoo-hoo and took a sip, spilling some of it on his white T-shirt. When Mank looked down at the stain, he was wearing a chocolate milk mustache. He licked his lips and frowned up, holding up his stained shirt and looking at it.

"Fuck, man!" Mank complained.

Korey made a quick hand to hand exchange with a nappy-headed crack fiend, who was wearing a sleeveless jean jacket and dirty sweatpants. Korey watched as the junkie glanced at his off-white rocks before stuffing them inside his pocket and strutting across the street, eyes bucked and arms swinging. Once Korey seen old boy going on about his business, he shoved the crumbled-up bills inside his Dickies and looked across the street at his right-hand man.

Korey threw his head back like, *what's up?* "What up, nigga?"

"I spilled this shit all over my T. Shit!" Mank pulled off his T-shirt and folded it up, tucking it into his left back pocket. He then went on with drinking his chocolate beverage.

"Yo, it's stupid hot out here. And it doesn't help that shit is slow too." Korey pulled a black bandana out of his left back pocket, folded it and dabbed the beads of the sweat from off of his forehead. He then tucked the bandana into his back pocket. "How many you got left?"

"Six." He told him how many dime-sized crack rocks he had left on him. "How about chu?" he asked, as he took another sip from his bottle of Yoo-hoo.

"Shit, eight."

"We damn near rocking the same boat."

At that moment, the youngstaz' attention was taken by a luxury vehicle flying up the street toward them, T.I.'s "Jefe" pumping from its speakers. Korey and Mank's eyes were locked on the whip which turned out to be a soft gray 2019 Mercedes-Benz S 600. The Benz whipped past Korey and Mank, screeched to a halt and came back in reverse. It stopped before Mank, who went for his waistline, along with Korey who was jogging over to him. The youngstaz dropped their hands at their sides once they saw a familiar face, with his arm hanging out of the driver's window, jewels shining.

"Damn, my nigs, don't shoot! It's just us, Zack and Joshua." The driver, Zack, chuckled with a smile. He was the shorter of the two. He stood five foot seven and had a big ass head, which was designed in cornrows. As of now, he was wearing a Chicago Cubs fitted cap cocked to the side and a matching jacket. When he said his name, the darker, taller, Joshua leaned forward so Korey and Mank could see him and smiled, throwing his head back like, *what's up?* Half of a smoldering blunt was wedged between his fingers. He was wearing a black mink hat and what the youngstaz assumed was a matching mink vest. "What cha'll niggaz doing out here, bruh?" Zack tapped his right-hand man, Joshua, and they jumped out of the Benz, leaving that beautiful bitch parked dead smack in the middle of the ghetto running, like there wasn't any car thieves or crackheads wandering around to steal it.

As Zack and Joshua were walking toward Korey and Mank, the youngsta couldn't help clocking the heavy jewelry they had on. Zack was wearing a platinum Jesus head and a crucifix, a platinum AP Rolex and a bracelet with small crucifixes hanging from it. His man, Joshua, was wearing a platinum name piece, which spelled out "JOSHUA" and a presidential Rolex with a black face. His pinky ring was fat as fuck with a black diamond at its center. It was safe to say that these niggaz was getting money—lots of it.

"What chu think we're doing?" Korey asked, like Zack already knew what kind of time he and Mank was on.

"Man, y'all young niggaz still out here serving?" Zack laughed as he dapped up Korey and Mank.

Mank shrugged and said, "My niggaz, if you don't knock our hustle, then we won't knock yours."

"I feel you, big homes, but if you tryna shine like me and mine," Zack began pulling up his sleeves showing off his jewels and then his chain, alongside Joshua, "That nickel and dime hustling fa sho not gon' get chu there, you feeling me?"

86

Zack and Joshua smiled and continued to flex on the young niggaz.

"Me and my nigga Mank ain't never been no haters so we salute cha'll." Korey saluted Zack and Joshua like they were sergeants. "We see y'all out here getting to the money."

"Fa sho, fa sho," Mank nodded. "It seems like y'all niggaz blew up overnight. I mean, what's it been, two, three years?" Mank glanced at Korey to confirm, but he shrugged and took the blunt from behind his ear, putting fire to its tip and blowing out a big ass cloud of smoke.

"Not even a full year, big homies," Zack assured him. "We're out here on our thug thizzle, going hard in the paint for ours. You see what dedication and determination get chu." He nodded back to the Benz that was idling in the middle of the street. "And that ain't shit but my Thursday car, my nig."

"Yep. My nigga was just taking me to pick up my shit," Joshua said as he took the blunt from Korey as he offered it.

"Oh, yeah? What chu whipping my nigga Josh?" Korey asked curiously.

"Drop top, seven series Beamer, baby. Right now, it's getting that chameleon paint job onnit and white leather interior."

"Sheesh! You getting that bitch right for the summer, huh?" Korey inquired.

"And you know this, man," Joshua said like Smokey in *Friday*.

"If y'all niggaz doing so good, then spread the wealth. Look out for your niggaz, put us on," Korey insisted as he blew smoke out from his nose. Korey, Mank, Zack and Joshua had known one another since high school. Zack and Joshua was one year older than them, but they used to kick it together tough. That was until Zack and Joshua dropped out of school and took it to the streets. Just like Korey and Mank, they started off petty hustling, but then they stepped it up to jacking dope boyz. This was how they amassed their small ghetto fortune. This paid for their lifestyle and allowed them the luxury of stunting and fronting in the middle of the hood.

"Put chu on?" Zack's eyebrows rose.

"Yeah, put us on. We're all homies here, right? Look out for yo brethren."

"Look, we usually get down on our own, but I may have something coming up that I can put chu lil' niggaz on to. Just lemme holla at my mans right quick." Zack tapped Joshua and motioned for him to follow him over to the Benz. Korey and Mank watched as they chopped it up for a minute before walking back over to them. The youngstaz looked Zack and Joshua over, wondering what their verdict was going to be.

"Aight, we're gon' give y'all lil' niggaz a shot, gemme yo math and I'll get up witchu when it's time to make that move." He pulled out his cell phone and programmed Korey and Mank's telephone numbers into his jack. "Cool. I'll get up witchu niggaz soon." Zack and Joshua exchanged daps with Korey and Mank before hopping back inside the Mercedes Benz and pulling off. Looking down the street at the Benz, Korey and Mank saw the license plate which read "PAID."

The next day

A MAC truck flew up the road, leaving debris in its wake, country music pumping from out of its windows. Its driver, Jericho, was behind the wheel singing along to a tune playing from out of its speakers. Jericho was a burly white man who rocked a baldhead and a bushy, auburn beard. He was wearing a baseball cap and a sleeveless plaid shirt, a black leather, spiked band was around his right wrist. As he nodded his head to the beat and crooned, he looked to his left side view mirror and saw a black 2001 Hondai, which was fixed up like a racing car zooming toward him. The vehicle rode beside him, with the driver honking its horn. The passenger, who was wearing a bandana over the lower half of his face, hung halfway out the window and pointed what looked like a long black machine gun at him. Jericho's eyes bugged and his thin lips peeled apart to form the letter O, he was so shocked. He tried to swerve the enormous truck from out of the line of the machine gun, but it was already too late.

Pop, pop, pop, pop, pop!

Bright yellow paint balls exploded upon hitting the driver's door of the Mack truck, scaring the living shit out of Jericho. He sighed with relief, realizing he hadn't been struck by real life bullets.

The passenger pulled himself back inside of the window and laughed his ass off, smacking the dashboard. "Hahaha-hahahahahahaha! We got 'em, we got 'em good, you should've seen my nigga'z face!"

Jericho's face turned beet red with embarrassment and rage. He grabbed his sawed off from the front passenger seat and pointed it out the window at the passenger. As soon as his ass saw it, his eyes lit up with terror.

"Oooooh, shit, mothafuckaz gotta gun, he's gotta gun! Pull off, pull off!" the passenger urged the driver and the Hondai sped off, flying up the road beside the yellow lines. As soon as Jericho pulled his sawed off back inside the window and turned around, he got a mini AK-47 shoved into his cheek. Instantly, his eyes became as big as golf balls and he swallowed the lump of nervousness inside his throat. His eyes darted to their corners and they found a nigga dressed in all black, wearing a ski mask with black sunglasses over his eyes. He was leaning over inside the window with that choppa jammed into the side of his face.

"Nigga, toss that sawed off outta the window 'fore I blow yo head off yo shoulders!" Zack, the masked up nigga said, voice dripping with deadly intent. Jericho tossed the shotgun out the window and it tumbled backwards down the road. "Now, pull this big mothafucka over!" he commanded. Jericho did like he was ordered. Once he did, Zack called him out of the truck through the passenger side door. "Jump down!" Zack called up to him, keeping his AK-47 on him. If he tried some funny shit, then he was going to pump him full of some hot shit.

"Look, man, I'm gonna do whatever you ask of me. Just don't shoot me, okay?" Jericho told him as he climbed down from out of the beast. At this time, the Hondai was pulling up behind them and the driver, Korey, and the nigga that had been mooning Jericho, Joshua, were hopping out of the car. They were both wearing earbuds in their ears, and looking like they meant some very serious business.

"Fall back, my nigga," Joshua said to Zack as he stepped before Jericho, who had his chubby hands up in the air, looking scared as shit. He watched Joshua with terror in his eyes, praying for the best but preparing for the worse. As soon as Zack stepped back, Joshua gave Jericho two vicious blows to his protruding gut and punched him in the jaw. The poor bastard's blood sprayed from his mouth and speckled the side of the truck. He then hit the ground hard, wincing. "That's for pulling that fonky ass gun on me, bitch!" Joshua stood over him with his balled fists at his sides. He spat on him and kicked him in his side causing him to groan. "Cuff his ass, man." He told Zack.

"New Booty, you do the honors!" Zack pulled two zip-cuffs from the small of his back and tossed them over to

Korey. Korey ran right over and zip-cuffed Jericho's meaty wrists behind his back and bound his ankles with the other zip-cuffs. Joshua and Zack then watched as Korey pulled a bandana out of his back pocket and tied it around Jericho's mouth, gagging him.

"Alright, time to crack this big bitch open and see our prize." Zack placed the strap of the AK-47 over his shoulder and approached the back of the truck, unlocking the shutter with the key he'd taken off of Jericho. Zack pulled up the shutter and found stacks and stacks of brown boxes before him labeled fragile. The boxes contained lamps. Zack whipped out his trusty box cutter and slit one of those babies open. He pulled a lamp out of one of the boxes and he tucked the box cutter into his back pocket. Joshua and Korey watched as he examined the lamp carefully before slamming it down at his booted feet, breaking it into clay shards. Using his booted foot, he sifted through the broken shards and exposed a kilo of cocaine. The kilo was stamped with a king's crown, which stood for King Rich. Zack picked up the block of coke and held it up, smiling. He looked from Joshua and Korey, saying, "Yeahhhh, we bouta be paid, motha-fuckaz!" Zack stashed the block between the boxes in the back of the truck. He then jumped down to the ground, dapping up Joshua and Korey happily. "Y'all help me put this fat fuck into the back of this truck so we can get back and unload this cargo."

"Alright, bet." Joshua tapped him and motioned for him to follow him over to Jericho. Together, they hoisted the big man up and placed him inside of the open shutter, locking it behind him. Zack and Korey rode back to the rally point in the Hondai while Joshua pushed the truck back, following them.

Tranay Adams

CHAPTER SIX

Mank paced back and forth beside the U-Haul truck, occasionally glancing at his watch. He found himself growing impatient waiting for Korey and the others to return. They were supposed to have been there twenty minutes ago. And now that they were late, he had a bad feeling that had his stomach doing summer salts.

Mank was well aware of the risk he was taking in being involved with the lick. The pros outweighed the cons. Shit, besides that, him and his right-hand man, Korey, were sick and tired of being the little niggaz in the game. You see, right now they were small fish in a big pond. They weren't even a blimp on the hood's radar. They wanted to be ghetto superstars, and the only way they were going to reach that status was through money—lots of money. They knew that with money came power and with power came respect. And they were willing to do any and everything they could to obtain it.

The waiting was wreaking havoc on Mank. He'd stop his pacing beside the U-Haul truck and placed his earbud inside his ear. He was about to hit up that nigga Korey and see what the fuck was taking them so long when he heard a car speeding in his direction. He turned around to see Zack and Korey pulling inside of the warehouse. Zack killed the engine and they hopped out, dapping up Mank.

"What the fuck took y'all niggaz so long, man? I thought y'all fools got popped or something." Mank looked between Korey and Zack.

"Fuck naw! There was an accident, so you know traffic was backed up on the highway," Korey told him.

"You worry too much, my young nigga. Shit was a piece of cake." Zack smiled and patted Mank on his back.

He then held up a pair of binoculars and looked through them. A big smile stretched across his face seeing Joshua coming up the road in that big ass MAC truck. "Here that nigga Josh come now, y'all niggaz move out the way so he can back this mothafucka in here."

Everyone moved out of the way and slipped on their individual pair of black leather gloves. They stood where they were, watching Joshua back in the MAC truck, listening to the enormous vehicle beep. Zack threw up a hand for Joshua to stop and he did. The lanky nigga then shut off the truck and threw open the door, climbing out of the beast. As soon as he jumped down, he ran to the rear of the vehicle and unlocked the shutter, with his keys. He lifted the shutter and revealed all of the boxes, as well as a gagged and bound Jericho.

"Fuck is up?" Mank frowned up and looked to Korey, wondering what was up with them bringing the truck driver along. He was expecting them to leave homie on the side of the road. So, it was off putting seeing the truck driver there.

"Chill, my nigga," Korey said, placing his hand on Mank's shoulder.

"Y'all niggaz bullshitting, man! Come on so we can hurry up and unload this shit, before we get pinched!" Joshua urged them all before pulling out the ramp and setting it on the ground. Zack made his way up the ramp and kicked Jericho out of the truck. The big man landed with a hard thud and the side of his head bounced off the pavement, causing him to wince. From there, Zack loaded four of the boxes on a dolly and rolled it down the ramp and over to the back of the U-Haul truck, where he proceeded to unload his cargo. Joshua did the same with a dolly of his own. Mank and Korey carried as many of the boxes as they could over to the

U-Haul. Together, they managed to unload everything in thirty-five minutes.

"Yo, what're we gon' do about him?" Korey looked to Jericho who was still lying on the ground where he'd been kicked, gagged and bound. He stared up at Zack with fear dripping from his eyes, wondering what the fuck he was going to do to him. With the question posed, Zack marched toward Jericho cradling his mini AK-47 and sprayed him twice, shocking Mank and Korey. Zack kicked Jericho once to make sure he was dead. Once he'd confirmed his kill, he dropped the AK-47 at the dead man's side and motioned for the youngstaz to follow him back to their respective vehicles.

That night

Joshua backed the U-Haul truck into Mank's backyard while Mank opened the garage door. Joshua hopped out and joined up with Mank, Korey and Zack. Together, they unloaded the boxes that contained the blocks of cocaine into the garage. While they were stashing the boxes inside the garage, unbeknownst to them, someone was peering through a worn hole inside the garage door, watching them sneakily.

"All these mothafucking bricks, dawg. Niggaz 'bouta be paid out the ass!" Joshua assured them all as they stacked the boxes in the corner.

"Man, you ain't never lied." Zack told him, sitting his box down on top of the one that Joshua had just sat down.

"Say, how're we gon' get rid of all this shit, bruh?" Korey asked curiously.

"Yeah, are we gon' break this shit down and sell it? Or get these bitchez off wholesale?" Mank inquired.

"We're gon' wholesale 'em but we're not selling 'em to anybody in Southern Cali. I'm sure the streets are gon' be

95

crawling with King Rich's people, looking for anybody selling mad work these next few days. So, our best bet is to sell these mothafuckaz to these niggaz my unc know outta town," Joshua informed them all.

"Good idea," Zack told him.

"Nigga, you ain't the only brains in the outfit." Joshua smirked. "I'ma take one of the bricks so they can getta taste of what we're working with," he claimed as he shoved one of the blocks inside a knapsack and closed it up, pulling it over his shoulders. When he turned around, he froze once he saw an eye staring in at them through the hole in the garage door. "What the fuck? Look!" Joshua pointed at the garage door with a surprised look on his face. Korey, Mank and Zack looked over their shoulder and saw the eye, which quickly disappeared once it knew it had been seen. Swiftly, Zack picked up the mini AK-47 and ran to the garage door, lifting it open. When he looked outside, he saw Tyrell's back as he fled down the driveway, hauling ass like he had a mothafucking lynch mob behind him.

Tyrell glanced over his shoulder as he ran, seeing Zack aiming the AK-47 at his back, he quickly threw up his hands.

"Oh, shit! Don't shoot, don't shoot, don't shoot!" Tyrell hollered out over and over again.

"Fuck!" Mank's eyes doubled in size once he realized who the fleeing man was. He looked back and forth between Tyrell and Zack. He rushed over to Zack and tilted the AK-47 up into the air just as it fired. An angry Zack shoved him aside and looked at him like he was crazy. "What the fuck is yo problem, bruh? That mothafucka knows where our shit is!"

"That's my sister's baby daddy, he ain't gon say nothing, dawg. I promise. Trust me!" Mank said with his hands held up in the air. Zack had turned his AK-47 on him.

Zack stared him down, contemplating on whether he should pop him or not. Having finally come to his decision, Zack lowered his AK-47 at his side. "If anything happens to our shit, you the first mothafucka I'm coming to smoke. Then, I'm popping his ass next. You got that?" He mad-dogged Mank, who still had his hands up, nodding yes. "Good. Now come on so we can finish putting this shit up."

***

"You've gotta be fucking shitting me!" Baby Boy said into his cellular as he paced the floor of his study, chains swinging from left to right.

"What's up?" Diabolic asked from where he was sitting before the desk. He and Baby Boy were reminiscing about old times with their father when he'd suddenly gotten a phone call.

Baby Boy looked up at Diabolic and held up one finger, signaling for him to give him a minute. Once he did this, Diabolic settled down in his seat and just watched his younger brother as he paced the floor, talking on his cell phone. While he watched him, he took the liberty to fire up the blunt he had behind his ear.

"I knew something was up. When did they find 'em? Is he still alive?" Baby Boy ran his hand down his face as he continued to pace the floor. When he looked at Diabolic and saw him smoking the bleezy, he snapped his fingers and motioned for him to pass it to him. Diabolic took a few drags off the blunt and passed it to his brother. He then blew smoke out of his nose and mouth as he continued to watch him. "Fuck! Look, keep me informed if you find out anything, okay? Alright, cool." He disconnected the call and passed the blunt back to Diabolic.

"What's the word?" Diabolic inquired with furrowed brows.

"One of our trucks got hit. One-hundred kilos, gone, can you fucking believe it?"

"Any leads?"

"Notta fucking one."

"I'ma hit the streets. See what I can dig up. I'm sure something will come up."

"I hope so." Baby Boy stared off into the distance thinking. "Never in a million years did I think someone would have the balls to hit us, never in a million years."

"Well, they did, baby boy. We aren't the only gangstaz in this town." Diabolic rose to his feet and snuffed out the ember of his blunt in the ashtray, abandoning it. "I'll get at chu later." Smoke continued to rise from the blunt that Diabolic left behind as Baby Boy thought about his ordeal. He didn't know who it was that snatched his shipment of yay, but once he found out the culprits responsible there was going to be hell to pay. That was for damn sure.

Later that night

Baby Boy pulled up inside of the Chevron gas station with Nipsey Hussle's "Grindin' All My Life" pumping from the speakers of his black and yellow, bumble bee Lamborghini. He pulled up to pump eight and pulled out a wad of dead presidents. He peeled off a one-hundred-dollar bill and handed it to the sexy young lady sitting in the passenger seat. She looked at him like he was crazy as he looked away, sucking on his cherry Tootsie Roll pop, bobbing his head. His forehead creased because he could see out of the corner of his eye that little mama hadn't gone. So he popped the sucker out of his mouth and turned down the volume of his music, looking her straight in the face.

"Is there a problem?" Baby Boy asked.

"Yes, it's not gentlemanly of you to have a lady pump your gas," she reasoned as she held up the Benjamin Franklin.

"I'm notta gentleman, I'ma gangsta...and you sure as fuck ain't no lady I've ever seen. You met me an hour ago and already done had my dick in yo mouth, yo pussy, and in yo ass. So, miss me with that bullshit, and get me fifty bucks on pump eight." He continued to suck on the Tootsie Roll pop and bob his head to the music as he turned it up. Little mama balled her face up and called Baby Boy "a bitch ass nigga" under her breath, but he couldn't hear it thanks to the volume being up so high. She then jumped out of the car and made her way toward the gas station, adjusting her skimpy skirt on her thick thighs. A moment later, a dull black van pulled up at the pump on the opposite side. Unbeknownst to Baby Boy, the back doors of the van opened and a couple of masked niggaz hopped out armed with choppaz.

The masked-up niggaz were visible in the side view mirror, but Baby Boy was oblivious to them. He was still nodding his head to the music and sucking on his Tootsie Roll pop. In fact, the only person he noticed was little mama who he'd given the gas money to. She sashayed across the lot, with her high heels clicking on the oil stained concrete. She balled up Baby Boy's change and threw it at him through the driver's window. He frowned up and looked down at the crumbled-up bills in his lap, picking them up. He looked into the side view mirror and watched homegirl pull a switchblade out of her purse, triggering its blade. She stuck the blade into the side of the car and dragged it alongside the vehicle as she walked toward the rear of it.

Baby Boy scowled and snatched the sucker out of his mouth, turning down the volume inside of his whip. He stuck his head out of the driver's window and hollered out, "Bitch, what the fuck is yo problem?" Homegirl continued to walk around the car, dragging the blade alongside of it as she held up the middle finger. At that moment, Baby Boy popped the locks on his door and hopped out. As soon as he did, the masked up niggaz moved in on him. His eyes widened with fear. He went to grab his gun from underneath the driver's seat, but the masked nigga at his rear busted him in the grill with the stock of his AK-47. The impact from the blow dropped him down to his hands and knees. Right then, little mama that had been carving up the side of Baby Boy's whip kicked him in his side and dropped him flat on his face.

"Punk ass mothafucka!" Little mama harped up phlegm and spit on Baby Boy. She then jumped in behind the wheel, slammed the door shut, cranked the car up and adjusted the rear view mirror. Next, she put it in gear and pulled off casually, leaving the masked up niggaz to deal with Baby Boy.

The masked-up niggaz grabbed Baby Boy under his arms and dragged him toward the back of the van, slimy ropes of blood hanging from his bottom lip. He moaned in pain as his eyes rolled to the back of his head. The masked-up dudes threw Baby Boy into the back of the van and jumped in behind him, pulling the double doors shut. The van pulled out of the gas station with the clerk looking out at them through the bulletproof window and picking up the telephone to call 911.

While Baby Boy was moaning in pain on the floor of the van, the masked-up dudes relieved him of his diamond chains, rings, AP Rolex, bracelets and those dead white guys he had in his pocket. When this was going on, the chauffeur, the only nigga that wasn't rocking a ski mask, looked over his shoulder then looked back through the windshield.

"We got 'em, y'all! We got that bitch-ass nigga," the chauffeur said excitedly.

"Yo, man, we gon' have to pop this nigga after he tells us where his stash at," one of the masked-up niggaz announced. "The last thang I want is this lick coming back on us."

"Man, this shit ain't gon' come back on us," the other masked-up nigga assured. "This nigga ain't 'bout it like his daddy was. You heard about all that dope them young ass niggaz got 'em for. The streets say he knew they did it and didn't do a goddamn thang about it. We're straight."

"Nah, fuck that! We aren't takin' any chances. Once we get this bag, we droppin' this nigga. And that's that. Agreed?"

"Agreed!" they said in unison.

One of the masked-up niggaz pulled out his cellular and checked his Instagram account. The other masked-up dude focused his attention up from looking out of the windshield like the chauffeur was doing. While this was taking place, Baby Boy's vision came into focus. He cautiously looked around. Realizing that he'd better take advantage of the situation, Baby Boy pulled a small knife from out of his sneaker. Using all of his might, he slammed the small blade into the booted foot of the masked man staring out of the windshield. The masked man dropped his AK-47 to the floor and Baby Boy picked it up, turning it on him.

Blatatatatatatatatat!

The masked-up nigga danced and fell against the wall of the van, sliding down, dead. Swiftly, Baby Boy spun around on his back and cut loose on the other masked-up fool. He danced as he was hit with some piping hot shit, too. Once he hit the floor of the van, Baby Boy stood over him and sprayed his ass again for good measure.

"Oh, shit!" the chauffeur blurted. He looked up into the rearview mirror and saw Baby Boy pointing the AK-47 at him, frowned up, still bleeding from the lower half of his face. The chauffeur saw the muzzle flashes of the AK-47 and the side of his head disintegrated. His blood, brain fragments, and skull splattered against the windshield and he hunched over the steering wheel. The van drifted off to the side and slammed into parked cars that were lined up and down the residential street. The horn of the vehicle blared continuously with the dead chauffeur's body lying against the horn. Baby Boy looked around at all of the niggaz he'd slumped. He then wiped his fingerprints from AK-47 and tossed that bitch aside. Afterwards, he grabbed all of his jewelry and put it back on, stuffing the money that was taken back inside his pocket. He picked up the cell phone the masked-up nigga was checking his Instagram account on and hit up Diabolic, popping open the back doors of the van. He jumped down into the street and took off running as fast as he could, looking from left to right. He saw the lights of nearby houses' coming on and people slowly starting to come out of their homes. His face began to shine as he ran and beads of sweat oozed out of his pores, running down his face and neck. He huffed and puffed, out of breath from running. Once he reached the end of the residential block, he began walking casually.

"Damn, nigga, 'bout time you picked up," Baby Boy said into the stolen cellular, touching the lower half of his face, fingertips coming away bloody. "Niggaz jacked me, fam! I need you to benda few corners and come get me. Nah, nah, I'm okay, just a lil' fucked up. But, I need you to scoop me up quick. I handled my business, if you know what I mean. Hold on." He looked up at the main street and the cross street that he was on. "I'm on Slauson and Western, finna head inside of that shopping center where that Food 4 Less is at. I'ma play the cut 'til you get here. Peace." He disconnected the call and jogged down the street, crossing the train tracks. The blue and reds lights of police car sirens shined on his him and the brick walls as police cars sped past him. The emergency vehicles were headed to the residential block where he'd just left three dead bodies at.

***

Diabolic ripped down the road with the headlights of his vehicle leading the way, leaving debris in his wake. Coming up the street he saw yellow tape, the red and blue flashing lights of police cars, and corner vans a distance ahead which made him slow down. He eventually stopped his car and looked around wondering where Baby Boy was hiding at. At that very moment, his cellular rung and Baby Boy told him that he was coming out. Soon after, Baby Boy ran out and snatched open the front passenger door, hopping in. Diabolic put the car in reverse and backed up, whipping the whip around, he then sped off in the opposite direction.

"What the fuck happened?" Diabolic asked, glancing back and forth between the windshield and Baby Boy, wondering what the fuck had happened to have left him looking so disheveled and battered.

Baby Boy told Diabolic exactly what happened and how he'd handled the situation. With the information that he was given, Diabolic now understood why the cops had shit taped off and why there were corner vans up ahead down the road.

"We've gotta find them fools that hit the truck, fam. We've got to. Now that niggaz know them fools got away with hitting my shipment, they think a nigga candy out here, bro. They think a nigga sweet, you feel me?"

"I got chu. I've been on that already and I gotta lead," Diabolic assured him. "Far as I know it's only one nigga, but we gon' make this bitch-ass nigga tell us who else was in on the lick."

"Bitch got away with my car too, fam. I loved that fucking car! Fuck!" Baby Boy slammed his fist into the door which rattled the front passenger window, which shown his reflection.

"Don't even wet that shit, bro. We're gonna get that shit back. Don't even trip. That's my word." Diabolic frowned up and he squeezed the steering wheel tight, biting his inner jaw. He was as hot as an oven. First, niggaz popped his daddy and now they were getting at his brother. He was beginning to think that niggaz thought that his family was pussy, and he couldn't have that. He was about to be on some real murder shit like that nigga Money Mitch in *Paid In Full*. Fools in the streets were about to recognize just how gangsta his mothafucking family really was. *Straight up!*

The next day

Korey and Mank kicked it out on the front porch passing a blunt between them, smoke wafting in the air. They were good and high when a crackhead they'd nicknamed Michael Jackson walked up, smiling from ear to ear. They'd named him Michael Jackson from the way he dressed. He almost always wore a black blazer over a white V-neck, flooding slacks and penny loafers. On top of that, they were in the 2000's and homie was still rocking a Jheri Curl, one which hung down to his back. All his ass was missing was the glittery glove and the signature dance moves.

"My young niggaz, what's good?" Michael Jackson asked.

"What up, M.J.? You got that for me?" Mank asked as he passed the blunt back to Korey.

"Yep. I got that and then some, big dawg. And I'm tryna cop some more." Michael Jackson looked around cautiously before pulling out a wad of wrinkled dead presidents, licking his thumb and thumbing through the bills excitedly. When he did this, the youngstaz' eyes grew as big as light bulbs and they licked their lips thirstily because if Michael Jackson's smoked-out ass had that paper. Then that meant he was willing to spend and spend big with them.

"Go see what's that's about." Korey tapped Mank on the leg and he hopped up, going to see what Michael Jackson was talking about.

Korey watched as Mank approached the gate and got the money Michael Jackson owed him and chopped it up with him for a few minutes. Before he knew it, Mank ran back over to him jovially.

"Yo, nigga just said his grandmomma just died and she left him a big bag. He wanna buy all we got left," Mank said excitedly.

Korey snatched the blunt out of his mouth and blew out a cloud of smoke. "Nigga, you lying?"

Mank took the blunt out of Korey's hand and took a couple of puffs off of it. He blew out a cloud of smoke and handed the bleezy back to his main man, shaking his head. "Nigga, I'll never lie to you about getting money. Keep that nigga entertained until I come back. Don't let 'em go nowhere, I'm tryna make this sell, for real for real." He jetted up the steps and headed inside the house, leaving Korey to chop it up with Michael Jackson.

A smiling Mank made his way down the hallway, passing the bathroom where his sister was taking a shower. He opened his bedroom door and shut the door behind him, locking it. He pushed the mattress to the side and stuck his hand inside the hole he'd made inside the box spring to get the bag of crack he'd stashed. His face balled up with confusion when he didn't feel anything. That's when he stuck his face inside the stash spot. His brows crinkled when he didn't see shit inside of it.

"What the fuck?" Mank cussed to himself and got down on his knees, looking under the bed. He didn't see anything under the bed either, so he looked on the other side of the bed. Still, there wasn't shit there. Standing upright, he put his hands on his hips and looked around his bedroom, trying to remember if he put his stash somewhere else than his usual spot. He scratched his head as another look of confusion crossed his face. He decided to look inside his stash spot inside of his box spring again. There still wasn't jack shit inside there. Pissed off, he stormed down the hallway and busted in on his sister, inside of the bathroom, startling her.

"Nigga, can't chu kno—" Shavon said, but the words died in her throat. Little mama was in her purple bra and panties. She was in the middle of covering up her black eye and the hand impressions around her neck. Shavon's eyes were wide open and so was her mouth. Looking back and forth between her reflection in the medicine cabinet mirror and her little brother, she could see her injuries and she knew that he could too. So there would be questions of how she'd gotten them.

"Yo, what the fuck happened to yo face and yo neck?" Mank cupped his sister's face with one hand, turning it from side to side, getting a good look at her. Tyrell had done a real number on her.

106

"Nothing."

"Fuck you mean nothing? I know you didn't do the shit to yo self!"

"How you know that?"

"Did Latrell do this to you? 'Cause if he did, then that nigga dead! Don't nobody put they hands on my mothafucking sister! I don't play that shit!"

"It wasn't Latrell," Shavon answered, staring at her reflection, applying makeup to her face to hide her black eye.

"Then who?"

"Don't worry about it, Mank. I'm grown. I can handle it."

"Look, if you don't tell me who it was that laid hands on you, then I'ma assume it was big bro and me and that nigga gon' gun it out, straight up."

Shavon didn't say anything. She continued to apply makeup to her face. When Mank figured out she wasn't going to say anything, he got frustrated as fuck, and made to leave the bathroom.

"Fuck it! I'm finna go get my shit, and when that nigga get home, I'm popping his ass. Straight like that!"

"Okay, okay, okay! It was Tyrell, alright? It was Tyrell," Shavon told him with watery eyes.

"Is that who stole my stash too?" Mank asked her.

She responded by bowing her head and uttering, "Yes."

"On mommas, I'ma kill that smoked-out-ass mothafucka!"

"Yo, bro, what's up?" Korey came into the house with what was left of the blunt pinched between his finger and thumb. Mank gave him the rundown and his face frowned up. He looked Shavon over and became just as angry as Mank had. "Homie gotta die, it's that simple. Where that nigga at?"

"I don't know, but y'all can't kill 'em." Shavon said, wiping her eyes with her fingers and thumb.

"Kill who and for what?" Latrell asked as he suddenly appeared in the bathroom's doorway. He looked at the youngstaz and then Shavon. He looked like an angry pit bull once he saw his boo, Shavon's face. He approached her, curling his finger under her chin and turning her face from left to right, examining it carefully. "Who did this?"

"That nigga Tyrell, bro. That mothafucka broke up in here, stole my shit, and put the beats on sis. And she's talking about letting that shit ride. I don't know about you, but if she think I'ma let this shit slide, then she got me fucked up."

"She got both of us fucked up, bro. That's my sister too. And ain't nobody 'bouta be bringing harm to her while I'm around and not get touched." Korey's face balled up with anger.

"So you got my back?" Mank asked.

"You ain't even gotta ask." Korey dapped him up.

"Come on." Mank headed out of the bathroom.

"Hold up. I'm coming witcha'll." Latrell walked out of the bathroom, with Shavon coming up behind him, begging them to let things with Tyrell be. Neither of them niggaz were hearing it though. Payback was a mothafucka and that nigga Tyrell was about to meet him.

"Yo, M.J., I ain't got nothing, dawg. When I re-up, I'ma fuck witchu though," Mank told Michael Jackson as he walked out of the house.

"Sho you right, big dawg." Michael Jackson went on about his business. Mank was a mothafucking fool if he thought Michael Jackson was going to sit on his money until he got some more drugs. Fuck no! He was going to go see someone else about his habit.

"If we gon' do this then we're gonna needa car," Latrell told the youngstaz.

"Don't worry about the car. I got us faded, just needa lift to get one," Korey replied.

"Cool."

"Please, y'all, just leave Tyrell be! Let this shit go, I'm begging you," Shavon shouted from the front porch of the house, tears streaming down her cheeks and shit. Seeing that the boyz were ignoring her, Shavon raced back inside of the house to get dressed and try to stop them before it was too late.

CHAPTER SEVEN

It was summer and the sun was beaming like crazy, so it was hot as fuck outside. It was summertime so niggaz were known to be tripping. It could have been the season, or niggaz just had a chip on their shoulder. Regardless of the reason, in the hood, around this time, bodies were known to drop like flies.

Although it was broad daylight, Latrell and the youngstaz didn't give a fuck. They were on a mission. That nigga Tyrell had fucked up and touched their queen, Shavon, so he had to pay—in blood. Latrell was behind the wheel of the car they'd secured earlier that day. Korey was an expert when it came to snatching whips. It didn't matter what make or model a car was, if it could be driven then he could get it. Shiiiiit, he'd been stealing cars ever since grade school for joy rides.

"I think that's him right there," Korey said from the passenger seat, pointing at the windshield.

"Where?" Mank sat up in the backseat and hung his head over the front seats, trying to get a good look through the windshield.

Latrell slowed the car down and looked closely, narrowing his eyelids into slits. "I see 'em. To the left, walking up the block, pushing that basket fulla shit."

"Now, I see 'em," Mank said, having finally spotted Tyrell. "Mow his bitch ass down, bro."

Latrell mad-dogged Tyrell as he made his way up the sidewalk, revving up the engine of his vehicle. His car skirted off, burning rubber down the street, leaving exhaust smoke and tire prints behind. The sound of the whip drew Tyrell's attention over his shoulder and he whipped his head around. His eyes bulged and his mouth dropped open seeing

111

Latrell in the car speeding after him. Right then, Tyrell abandoned his shopping cart and took off running down the street.

"Don't let that mothafucka getta way, bro!" Mank said with a frown fixed on his face.

"I got this, this nigga ain't going anywhere. Trust me." Latrell assured him with concentration and determination written across his face.

Vroooooom!

Latrell's whip ripped up the street, leaving debris in its wake. Tyrell ran as hard and as fast as he could, constantly looking over his shoulder, huffing and puffing out of breath. He was trying to flee with his life, but it didn't seem like he was going to be successful, at least not in this moment.

BUNK!

Tyrell flew over the windshield of Latrell's whip and traveled over the full length of it, banging off the trunk and landing hard on the ground. He lay there with his eyes rolled to their whites, wincing, and breathing hard, slowly trying to peel his self from off of the pavement.

"Come on, Mank!" Korey hopped out of the car and called after his homeboy. He was en route to put the beats on that nigga Tyrell's ass for what he did to Shavon. He looked at her like his big sister, so she was family. As good as blood to him.

Korey ran around the corner and kicked Tyrell in his side causing him to howl like a wounded dog. Mank came up from behind him and stomped Tyrell in the head, making his dome bounce off the ground like a Spalding basketball. After that, Latrell climbed out of the car and walked around to the rear of it, watching as the youngstaz stomped, kicked and pounded Tyrell's ass out. Them young, thug ass niggaz had Tyrell bleeding from his nostrils and mouth. His nose was busted and so were his lips. A lump had formed off center on his forehead.

"Bitch-ass nigga, gon' put his hands on my mothafucking sister, and take my shit! Oh, you had this ass whipping coming!" Mank shouted, looking like an angry, barking German shepherd about the face. He was kicking Tyrell so viciously and fast that his legs looked like blurs.

"Oofs" and "Owws" escaped Tyrell's lips as kick after kick and stomp after stomp rained down upon him.

"Where the fuck is our shit, nigga?" a pissed off Korey asked as he held the trunk of Latrell's vehicle, kicking the living shit out of Tyrell. While all of this was taking place, Latrell was leant up against his car smoking a cigarette, watching. Once he looked up and saw there wasn't anybody outside observing what was taking place, he dropped the Joe down to the pavement and mashed it out underneath his sneaker.

"I smoked it all with yo mother after I fucked her up the ass!" Tyrell managed to say between kicks. This made Korey madder than he was before and he kicked him across the chin, dropping his head to the asphalt. He lay there moaning in agony, eyes rolled to the back of his head as he bled out from his mouth.

"Alright, that's enough! Y'all drag his ass over inside of the alley." Latrell pulled out his blower and cocked that shit. He followed Mank and Korey as they grabbed Tyrell underneath both arms and dragged his skinny black ass over inside the alley, his knees coming across broken glass and loose garbage. They held him up against the gate of a business that had been shut down for quite some time.

Latrell looked Tyrell dead in his eyes just like he did every nigga or bitch before he killed them. His nose was scrunched up and his lips were peeled back in a sneer. Tyrell was in pain and bleeding in the face, barely conscious. He could see his reflection in Latrell's pupils.

"Fuck you waiting on, nigga? For me to give you a kiss?" Tyrell puckered up his lips and then he made kissing noises. Right after that, he was busting up laughing. With a grunt, Latrell cracked him at the top of his skull with the butt of his handgun, which dropped him down to his hands and knees.

Latrell looked down at Tyrell with hatred burning in his eyes as he lowered his gun at his face. Tyrell looked at him with no fear whatsoever pumping through his heart and veins, waiting for the shot that would end his life forever. Mank and Korey looked back and forth between Latrell and Tyrell waiting to see exactly what would happen next.

"Fuck yo life, nigga!" Latrell said to Tyrell and pulled the trigger.

Boc!

"Oooomf!" Latrell winced in pain as he was tackled to the ground by Shavon. She grabbed his gun and scrambled to her feet.

"Tyrell, run!" Shavon shouted out to the man she'd had a child with at one time. Tyrell took off down the alley hauling ass. When Mank and Korey tried to go after him, Shavon popped a hot one into the sky and then turned her gun on them, moving it back and forth between them.

"What the fuck is your problem?" Latrell said as he scrambled to his feet and brushed the dirt from off his jeans.

"I'm sorry, y'all, but I cannot let cha'll kill 'em," Shavon said after Tyrell disappeared down the alley. She then ejected the magazine out the bottom of the handgun and threw it upon the roof. Next, she handed the handgun back to Latrell, who was looking at her ass like she was crazy.

"Why the fuck not? He kicked yo ass and ran off with me and Korey's shit." Mank stepped to his sister, mad-dogging her.

"I know. And I'ma pay y'all back for all he took," Shavon swore.

"Sis, what kinda hold does this nigga have on you? Why don't chu want us to put 'em in the dirt?"

"Because regardless of whatever he's done, he's still JaQuawn's father."

When she mentioned her deceased child's name, Latrell, Mank and Korey bowed their heads, thinking of the boy and his tragic death which was truly, truly sad.

"Outta love and respect for JaQuawn, please leave Tyrell be. I'm asking you not as yo woman, or your sister, but as a mother," Shavon told them, eyes on the brink of tears.

Mank took a breath and he massaged his nose, nodding, he said, "Okay, sis, you got it."

Shavon looked to Korey. "Alright. If that's how you want it," Korey conceded.

Shavon looked to Latrell.

"I'ma let his ass slide this time, but," Latrell held up his index finger, "if he kicks up anymore shit, then that's his ass."

"Agreed," Shavon told him.

Right then, the sound of police car sirens filled the air and they all took off running. Shavon hopped into her car and peeled off and so did Latrell. His cell phone rang and vibrated so he answered it, having seen that it was Diabolic.

"Alright. Just gemme like a half-hour, I've gotta drop off my people. After that, I'll slide through."

Diabolic disconnected the call without saying goodbye, coming off rude as fuck. "Bitch-ass nigga." Latrell slid the cellular back inside his pocket.

***

Whitney was down inside the basement getting high as a bitch when she heard four hard ass knocks on the basement window, which startled her. Crack pipe in one hand and lighter in the other, Whitney rose from the mattress where she was sitting Indian style and slowly walked over to the window, blowing smoke out of her nose and mouth. She lowered her head and peered up at the window through narrowed eyelids, trying to figure out who it was with that ghetto ass knock.

"Who is it?" Whitney asked loudly.

"It's me!" the person responded. All she could make out was their silhouette.

"Who the fuck is me, nigga?"

"It's me, baby! Tyrell! Niggaz fucked me up, I'm hurting, boo."

"Shit! Come to the door, I'ma let chu in," Whitney told him as she stashed the crack pipe and the lighter inside of her shirt pocket.

"Where's Ms. Pearl?"

"She's at a card game at Mrs. Carol's house. She won't be back for a minute.'"

"Okay."

"Alright. I'm finna be on my way up."

Whitney hurried up the basement's staircase and into the living room where she opened the door for Tyrell. As soon as she did, she couldn't help noticing how Tyrell looked like he'd went a few rounds with Mike Tyson. He fell right into her arms, breathing harshly and wincing in pain. Mank and Korey had beaten the brakes off of that ass. The beat down he'd gotten would be etched in his mind forever.

"I think—I think my mothafucking ribs are broken, bae. Them niggaz whipped my natural black ass."

Whitney dragged him over to the couch and laid him down. She then shut the door behind them and locked it. "Who? Who beat chu up?" Whitney inquired as she ducked off in the kitchen and got a butcher's knife out of the wooden block on the island. She returned to the living room where she peered out of the curtains, hoping that no one had followed Tyrell home. The last thing she wanted to do was bring heat to where she was living.

"Shavon's lil' brother and his homeboy, then her man smacked me upside the head with his pistol. Nigga was finna do me 'til Shavon showed up and saved my ass," Tyrell told her from where he lay stretched out on the couch, touching his face and coming away with bloody fingertips. He grimaced every time he touched his fingers to his face because his shit was sore all over.

"You think they followed you back here?" Whitney turned away from the window and looked at Tyrell, still holding the butcher's knife. Before he could answer, she was unlocking the door and checking the outside. There wasn't anything going on out of the ordinary out there so she shut the door back and locked it, chaining it up.

"Nah, nah, they didn't follow me back here. Shavon kept them off of me. She busted a shot in the air and then she turned her gun on 'em."

Whitney sat the butcher's knife down on the coffee table and got down on her knees beside the couch, placing Tyrell's hand inside of hers and caressing it gently, looking up at his bruised and bleeding face.

"For real? Why in the fuck would she do something like that when you stole from her?" Whitney asked with a furrowed brow.

"I don't know," he shrugged, "But, if I hadda guess, I'd say it had something to do with me being JaQuawn's father. I'm sure had it not been for that, then she would have let Latrell paint that wall with my brains."

"Well, whatever her reasoning being, thank God for it." She kissed him on his hand. "Now, come on, I'ma help you get undressed and get into a hot bath. Afterwards, I'ma clean up those wounds of yours."

Whitney grabbed Tyrell by the hand and led him inside the bathroom where she had him sit on the commode while she drew him a hot bath. Once she twisted the dials off, she helped him take off his clothes, underclothes, socks and sneakers. She dipped her hand into the water to check its temperature and it was just right. Afterwards, she helped Tyrell inside of the tub. He laid his head back against the tiled wall and exhaled with relief, shutting his eyelids. The hot water was soothing and provided therapy for Tyrell's aching body. While he was relaxing, Whitney went about the task of cleaning the dry blood from his face. She stopped for a moment and gave him the crack pipe and the lighter out of her shirt pocket.

"Take a few hits of that, it'll help you feel better." Whitney referred to the crack inside the pipe she was smoking earlier when he knocked on the basement's window, disturbing her. She then went back to cleaning his wounds and then washing him up.

Tyrell took a few pulls from the crack pipe and blew out big ass clouds of smoke. He started feeling good then. Whitney was right. That shit did make him feel better.

After Whitney finished washing Tyrell up, she helped him out of the tub and dried him off while he continued to get high. She then helped him inside of a pair of boxer briefs and slipped his feet into a pair of corduroy house shoes.

They found themselves down in the basement lying on the mattress and sharing the crack pipe. Tyrell lay on his back with one hand behind his head, staring up at the ceiling in deep thought.

"Them niggaz got me fucked up if they think I'ma let that shit ride though, Whit. A nigga wasn't always a fucking crackhead. Once upon a time, I was one of the biggest gangstaz this city has ever seen. And I'ma remind niggaz of that for real, for real."

That night

Zack sat on the sofa in the living room, rolling his self a blunt as he watched *Belly* on the flat screen television set. He licked the bleezy closed and used the flame of a lighter to seal it shut. Once he'd done this, he stuck the Swisher between his fat lips and put fire to the tip of it. He sucked on the end of the blunt and gave birth to small smoke clouds. He tossed the Bic lighter upon the coffee table and sat back against the sofa, taking casual pulls from the overgrown Swisher. It wasn't long before his eyes became glassy and red webbed and he looked like he was falling asleep. Smoke wafted around him as he continued to indulge in the best Kush he'd ever had and slid his hand inside his pants, massaging himself.

Zack was so engrossed in his smoking that he hadn't noticed the embers drop into his lap. As soon as he felt them he danced in his seat and smacked them off his lap. Jumping to his feet, he looked down at the holes in the lap of his Dickies, shaking his head, frowned up.

"Fuck! I done burnt fucking holes in my pants and shit!" Zack complained as he switched hands with the smoldering blunt. He became as stiff as a surfboard once he felt cold steel press against the back of his dome piece. His eyes shot to their corners and he dropped the blunt from between his fingers.

"Strip, nigga!" Diabolic ordered from behind him.

"Nigga, fuck you!" Zack spat back defiantly.

"I said, strip!" Diabolic roared and popped a cap in his ass, causing him to stumble forward and hold his aching buttock, wincing. Zack looked at his gun, which was lying on the coffee table. He thought about going for it but what Diabolic said next made him think again. "You're young, dumb and 'bouta be fulla some hot shit if you thinking about reaching for that strap, kid! Now strip like the fuck I said!"

"Fuck you!" Zack hollered aloud, still holding onto his G-card.

"Oh, yeah?" Diabolic smiled wickedly.

"Yeah, nigga, fuck you!" Zack looked over his shoulder.

Diabolic placed his gun beside Zack's ear and pulled the trigger.

Boc!

At that moment, Zack's eyes became as big as golf balls and an eerie siren sounded off inside his ears. He lost his balance and crashed down on top of the table, breaking it in half. He squeezed his eyelids shut again and again as he winced, trying to fight back what felt like a dizzy spell. He crawled and continuously fell to the floor while en route to his gun. He picked it up and fell on his back, pointing his gun. At the end of his blower, he found Diabolic and two goon ass niggaz. The room was tilting back and forth to him, so he couldn't draw a bead on Diabolic, but that didn't stop him from opening fire.

Splocka, splocka, splocka, splocka!

The bullets flew over Diabolic and his goons' heads, shattering a lamp and a vase across the living room. While the bullets were flying, Diabolic and his goons didn't even budge. Nah, they laughed at his young ass. Pretty soon, Zack dropped the gun. Diabolic pulled the black bandana down from the lower half of his face. Scowling, he spoke to the goons posted up on either side of him.

"Y'all beat the shit outta this nigga and drag 'em down in the basement." Diabolic walked down the hallway and made a turn into the bedroom. A while later, he returned with white bed sheets tied together, watching his goons stomp and kick the living shit out of Zack. Once they were finished handing him his ass whipping, the goons dragged him toward the door of the basement. He was bloody faced and nearly naked, wearing blood stained boxers and one sneaker.

Diabolic followed behind his goons as they drug Zack down in the basement, bumping his head on every single step along the way. Once they reached the landing, they pulled him over to the center of the basement floor and pulled the drawstring, restoring light to the space. Diabolic had his goons hold Zack up while he used his black bandana to tie his wrists behind his back. He then made the sheets into a homemade noose and looped it around Zack's neck. Next, he threw the sheet over a beam in the ceiling and had one of his goons pull it until the young nigga, Zack, was standing on the balls of his feet, dripping blood from his chin.

"My young nigga, you're up Shit's Creek withoutta paddle. There's only one way you're gonna be able to save yourself, and that's by telling me everything I want to know," Diabolic told him straight up.

"I'm not telling you jack shit, so kiss my black ass!" Zack spat blood into Diabolic's face, speckling it. Diabolic shut his eyelids just as the blood splattered against his face.

He smiled wickedly and wiped it away with the sleeve of his shirt.

"Everybody wants to be a gangsta," Diabolic said and popped a hot one into Zack's kneecap which caused him to throw his head back and wail aloud, veins forming all over his head. Zack threw his head back screaming louder and louder, spit flying from his lips.

"Aaaaaah! Aaaaah! Aaaah!" Zack's head jerked from left to right and he thrashed around in excruciation. When he finally settled down, he bowed his chin to his chest and breathed huskily. Blood poured out of the hole in his kneecap and dripped on the floor.

"Now, I wanna know where that shipment of yay is, and I wanna know where the mothafucka at that helped you lift it," Diabolic demanded wearing a dead serious expression.

"I guess—I guess you're hard of hearing, homeboy, so I'll tell yo monkey ass again! Kiss my black ass!" a mad-dogging Zack fired back.

Diabolic started laughing. He looked back at his goons and they started laughing too. You'd think they'd just heard the funniest shit in the world with the way they were carrying on.

Diabolic's eyebrows arched and his nose scrunched up. He whipped his head back around to Zack and popped one in his other kneecap and in his shoulder. The young nigga, Zack, hollered aloud again, feeling the fire rip through his body. He was aching, in pain, and wished Diabolic would just kill him and get it over with. You see, Zack wasn't about to tell Diabolic were the coke was and he sure as shit wasn't about to roll over on his niggaz.

"Grrrrrrrr!" Zack's nostrils flared and he clenched his jaws hard, causing them to pulsate. He was fighting back the pain he felt in his freshest wounds.

"You see what all that tough talk get chu? Huh?" Diabolic yelled in his face, holding up his gun. He then tucked his blower at the small of his back and motioned for Latrell to come to his side, keeping his eyes on a gritting Zack. "Lemme get that." He wiggled his fingers and Latrell came out of his belt with the late King Rich's cane. He placed the cane down in Diabolic's palm. As soon as Diabolic got the cane, he whirled it around like a baton.

"You see this cane, youngsta?" Diabolic asked Zack as he held the cane in both hands. "It belonged to the realest nigga to have ever breathed air—Rich Greene, my old man. You wanna know a secret? It doubles as a katana," he unsheathed the katana from the opposite half of the cane. He then held up the sword. A gleam swept up the length of the blade and it twinkled at its tip. Diabolic admired the blade, his reflection shown on it. "Legend has it that Pops beheaded one hundred men with this mothafucka. How true that is, I don't know, but I'll tell you what I do know for sure. If you don't tell me what I wanna know, I'ma take you apart with it." He placed the katana under Zack's chin and tilted his head upwards. Zack squeezed his eyelids shut and swallowed the lump of fear in his throat. For the first time that night, he was actually afraid. "So, where's the shipment, and where's the fuck that hit the truck witchu, nigga?" Diabolic tilted his head to the side as he eyeballed Zack closely. He was sure the young nigga was going to tell him what he wanted to know now.

Zack peeled his eyelids open and looked Diabolic dead in his eyes. He scowled and bit down hard on his bottom lip, saying, "You should really invest in some hearing aids, bruh! Again, kiss my black ass, you fucking faggot!"

"I salute cho G," Diabolic saluted Zack's courage. He then drew the katana back and swung it forward. It whistled through the air, and sliced off Zack's right ear and then his left ear. The bloody severed ears fell to the basement floor. "Gaaaahhhh! Aaaahhhh!" Zack hollered and hollered, blood sliding down both sides of his neck.

"You wanna tell me now, tough guy, huh? You wanna tell me now?" Diabolic cupped his hand around his ear and leaned forward, listening closely.

"Fuck youuuuu! Suck my dick, bitch!"

Diabolic grabbed Zack by the lower half of his face so hard that his lips puckered up. He then drew the katana back and jabbed him repeatedly in his torso, spilling blood on top of blood on the floor, slicking it wet. Seeing blood on his shoes, Diabolic's anger flared up and he jumped up, kicking a dead Zack upside the head. He then took his black bandana from around Zack's wrists and wiped his hands with it. Then, he wiped off the katana's blade and its handle.

"Let's go." Diabolic sheathed the katana and stuck it inside his belt, as he walked toward the staircase. As he, Latrell and the goons walked through the living room, they heard a ringing and vibrating cell phone. Diabolic's eyes scanned the floor until they landed on Zack's torn-up, bloody Dickies. He fished through the pockets of the Dickies until he found the cellular. He opened the device and found a text message from Joshua.

Yo, I thnk I fnd us a buyer, wya?

A serious expression spread across Diabolic's face seeing the text message. He knew then that Joshua was the other nigga involved in the stealing of the shipment of coke. Right then, Diabolic hit him back up.

'Bout 2 slide from this lil broad house, wya my nig?

When Zack's cell phone rung and vibrated with a new text message from Joshua, Diabolic smiled devilishly.

CHAPTER EIGHT

Joshua sat on the arm of the couch watching Nefarious split open the brick of yay he'd taken out of Mank's garage. He observed the older, muscular man chop up the coke with playing cards until it was smooth, before making a thin line of it to snort. Once Nefarious had finished making the line of coke, he rolled up a blue-face, one-hundred-dollar-bill to snort the line up his right nostril. As soon as the powdery substance hit him, Nefarious dropped the rolled up one-hundred-dollar-bill and threw his head back, pinching his nose so that he wouldn't sneeze and fuck up his high. He felt an icy drip at the back of his throat. He swallowed and brought his head back down. His eyes were glassy and his nose was a little runny with clear snot. Nefarious blinked his eyelids continuously and flicked his nose.

"Mannnn," Nefarious looked down at the package of coke, pointing at it. "That shit right there is a fucking champion. Hit me like an uppercut from Mayweather or some shit."

"So you fucking with me?" Joshua asked him.

"Hell, yeah. How many you said you got again?"

"I gotta hunnit."

"How much you want for 'em?" Nefarious took the time out to light up a Newport and blew out a cloud of smoke.

"Look, I'ma mothafucking jackboy. I ain't no dope boy, so, uh," Joshua massaged his chin as he thought of a price to hit Nefarious with. "Gemme twenty a piece for them bitchez, and you can roll off with 'em."

Nefarious nodded his head as he sucked on the square, putting the lighter back inside his pocket as smoke wafted around him. "Cool, cool, cool, I can fuck with that. Just lemme holla at boss-man, I'm sure he gon' fuck witchu

125

'cause he been looking for a come up, and this shit perfect. I got cho math so I'ma holla at 'em tonight and make sure he gets back at chu tomorrow. Cool?"

"Cool," Joshua and Nefarious rose to their feet at the same time.

"Don't sell them bitchez to no one else, man. I'm serious," Nefarious said as he buttoned the center of his black blazer which he wore over a white V-neck. His big bald-headed ass looked like Terry Crews from the *Everybody Hates Chris* TV show.

"They ain't going anywhere, my nigga. I fucks witchu the long way."

"Cool."

"Come on. I'ma walk you outside."

Joshua unlocked the door and he and Nefarious walked outside, walking down the steps. They chopped it up some more as they treaded across the front lawn, en route to the gate where Nefarious's Cadillac was waiting at curbside. As they exited the front yard, unbeknownst to them, a Dodge Charger crept up the block, heading in their direction.

Nefarious stepped out into the street and walked around to the driver's door of his Cadillac. He unlocked the door and looked up at Joshua. "Alright, my nigga, I'ma make sure my people get at…"

Skiiiiiirt!

Blocka, blocka, blocka, blocka!

The gunman hung out the front passenger window with a handgun with a long ass magazine, blasting at Nefarious's back and blowing bloody black holes through the front of him. His eyes were wide and lifeless as his mouth hung open. He dropped to the ground fast and dramatically. Joshua gasped and looked up, only to see the cold, hardened eyes of

126

Nefarious's killa over the bandana that covered the lower half of his face.

"Oh, shit!" Joshua hollered out as the gunman, Diabolic, turned his Glock with the extended magazine on him. Once he pointed the blower at Joshua and pulled the trigger, the handgun bucked wildly spitting rapid fire.

Blocka, blocka, blocka, blocka!

Joshua ducked low and threw his arms over his head to shield himself as he ran. He bent the corner of a house and made it inside an alley. The Dodge ripped up the alley behind Joshua with homeboy spitting flames at his ass, trying to lay him down forever. It was dark out so the only things that could be seen were the headlights of the Dodge, which were shining at the back of Joshua as he hauled ass up the path.

Blocka! Blocka! Blocka! Blocka!

"Aaahhhhh!" Joshua threw his head back and hollered out in excruciation, grabbing his thigh and limping as fast as he could to get away. "Grrrrrrr! Fuck!" When he glanced over his shoulder and saw the black Dodge Charger on his ass, he knew he was a goner, but he was still going to try to get away. "Haa! Haa! Haa! Haa!" Joshua continued to limp along and glance over his shoulder.

"Get back in! I'ma 'bouta run this cocksucka over." Latrell ordered from behind the wheel of the Dodge Charger. As soon as Diabolic pulled himself back inside the car, the distinct smell of gun smoke filled the interior. The over-whelming stench didn't bother them though. They were used to the odor, having been in plenty of firefights before.

Latrell floored the gas pedal and the Charger blew down the alley, rolling over Joshua and leaving him tumbling down the pavement. Once he finally stopped, he was bloody and had tire prints across his white T-shirt. He laid flat on his back, staring down the alley at the back lights of the Charger, blood running down into his eye, causing him to blink his eyelid rapidly. He swallowed the blood in his throat and lifted his hand, as if he was trying to get the driver to stop before he killed him.

"Is that mothafucka still alive?" Diabolic looked out the back window.

"Yeah, he's still alive," Latrell confirmed.

"I'll be right back." Diabolic jumped out of the whip and looked down both ends of the alley for witnesses. Once he didn't see any, he threw his hoodie over his head and pulled out a thick ass roll of silver duct tape, which he used to gag Joshua's mouth and bound his wrists and ankles. He then picked his tall ass up like he was his newly wedded wife and walked him back to the Dodge Charger, calling out to Latrell, "Pop the trunk so I can put this piece of shit in there!"

Once Latrell obliged Diabolic, he dumped Joshua's body inside the trunk and hopped into the front passenger seat. He lit up the blunt that was lying inside the ashtray as they pulled off, taking drags from it and blowing clouds of smoke out of the passenger window.

***

Diabolic stood before Joshua, whose body was chained against a pillar down inside the basement of a condemned house. He screwed the cap off a red gas can and tossed it aside. He then splashed and splashed Joshua with the can's contents until it was empty. Afterwards, he tossed the gas can aside and whipped out a silver Zippo lighter, triggering a blue flame with a yellowish tip. The illumination from the flame shined on a battered Joshua, Diabolic and the two goons standing on either side of them.

He watched as Joshua squeezed his eyelids shut and shook his head, blowing his nose as the overwhelming odor of gasoline burned his nostrils. Joshua gagged and huffed as the fumes of the flammable liquid invading his lungs, threatening to poison him. Fearful of losing his life, he squirmed around trying to get free.

"Now, you're gonna tell me where y'all hiding that shipment at, or yo bitch ass is going up in a burst of flames. Now, where the fuck is the shit at?" Diabolic bit down hard on his bottom lip as he scowled, smacking Joshua viciously across the face a few times. Each one of the blows caused gasoline to fly off of him, dashing on the floor. Diabolic followed up by pulling the gag down from Joshua's mouth to hear what he had to say.

"Fuck you! Fuck you, you mothafucka! I'm not telling you shit, so if you gon' kill me then kill me!" Joshua spat heatedly as gasoline dripped from his brows and he mad-dogged all of the goons in attendance. His chest rose and fell rapidly as he breathed, taking in the odor of the flammable substance.

Diabolic tossed the Zippo lighter at Joshua's drenched body and he instantly ignited. Diabolic walked off, leaving the youngsta screaming to high heaven and struggling to break free from the binding chains which rattled. Diabolic whipped out a bandana from his right back pocket and used it to wipe his hands of the drops of gasoline that stained them. After stuffing the bandana back into his right back pocket, Diabolic pulled out his cellular.

"Who are you calling?" Latrell asked Diabolic. He'd been waiting in the shadows the entire time Diabolic was interrogating Joshua.

"Baby Boy," Diabolic replied as they made their way up the staircase. "We got nothing, but the message will be clear. No one fucks with this family," Diabolic said into the cell phone.

"Good," Baby Boy said and disconnected the call.

***

Whitney played the corner, sucking on a cherry Tootsie Roll pop and adjusting the strap of her purse on her shoulder. She was wearing a form fitting white dress that left very little to the imagination and matching stilettos. Occasionally, she found herself pulling her dress down over her thighs as it continuously rose up, exposing the lower halves of her panty less buttocks. Feeling a cool breeze ruffle the hairs of her wig, Whitney walked over to a parked Nissan and looked into its passenger mirror. She popped the sucker out of her mouth and fixed her hair and adjusted her voluptuous boobs in her dress. Hearing a vehicle coming up behind her, she looked over her shoulder and saw a Toyota pickup truck nearing her.

Whitney hurried over to the corner as the Toyota pickup truck pulled up. She looked inside of the vehicle and saw a hefty, pink-faced white man wearing a fisherman's hat, undershirt and suspenders. When the white man saw Whitney, he smiled from ear to ear, boasting the gold crown on his front tooth. He motioned Whitney over to his truck and she smiled, making her way over to him, stooping down so he'd be able to see her face. She was all dolled up in makeup and her hair was laid to the gods. She knew she had to look right if she was going to catch any tricks.

Whitney popped the sucker out of her mouth and smiled at the white man, saying, "Hey, handsome, how are you doing tonight, baby?"

"I'm fine, beautiful, how about you?" the white man replied jovially.

"I'm great, lover. Now, it's sixty dollars for the bombest head in the world and two hundred for the best pussy in the universe. So, tell me what chu want, big poppa?" she licked her top lip seductively.

The white man undressed Whitney with his eyes and licked his lips hungrily, saying, "Oh, I want the full ride, gorgeous."

"You've just bought yourself a date, handsome." She snatched the door open and hopped into the passenger seat. "Pull around the corner here, baby."

"Alright, sweetness," the white man said.

Tyrell, who was wearing a black bandana over the lower half of his face, popped up on the driver's side of the white man's Toyota pickup truck, pointing a beat-up .44 Magnum revolver with duct tape around its handle in his face. "Hop yo fat ass up outta the car, and if you try some funny shit, I'ma slump you! That's on God and heaven! Now, get the fuck out, you fat mothafucka!" Tyrell raged as he unlocked the door and yanked that bitch open. He grabbed the chunky white man by the collar of his shirt and pulled him out of the whip roughly. He then shoved him up against the hood of the car and kicked his legs apart as he planted his hands on the vehicle. "Let's see what chu got, fat boy!" Tyrell ran through the white man's pockets leaving him with rabbit ear pockets inside out. He came up with two crumbled-up dollars and some loose change. "You better have more than this or I'ma pop you for wasting my time." Tyrell stuffed the dollars and change inside of his pocket.

Afterwards, he pulled his worn, black leather wallet from out of his back pocket and cracked it open. He smiled wickedly on one side of his mouth, once he saw his victim had a few blue-faced, one-hundred-dollar-bills. He yanked them shits out of his wallet and tossed the wallet over his shoulder, into the street. Next, he pulled the white man over and stuck his pistol so far inside his grill that he gagged on the bitch. Looking him square in the eyes, he said, "I want chu to run south until you reach the intersection. If you stop and look over yo shoulder then that's yo lily white ass, you got that?" With his eyes full of fright, the white man nodded, meaty, pink palms shivering. "Alright then, beat it!" Tyrell smacked the fisherman's hat off the man's head and kicked him in his ass as he ran away. He watched him haul ass down the middle of the street. Once he was halfway down the block, Tyrell pointed his revolver into the air and pulled the trigger. The chamber spun once and sparks flew from out of the scarred, black barreled pistol, sending a lone bullet high into the air. The sound of gunfire made the fleeing white man run that much harder, and caused Tyrell to double over laughing. He watched the white man for a moment before jumping in behind the wheel of the Toyota and peeling off in the opposite direction.

**

Worth pulled up in the parking lot of LaSalle's Italian Restaurant. He slid out from behind the wheel and jumped out, slamming the door shut behind him. He made his way toward the establishment hearing the sounds of violins and a sultry voice. Worth crossed the threshold of LaSalle's taking in the environment. The place was packed. The lights were dim. There were waiters and waitress moving back and forth across him with tantalizing entrees of Italian dishes that smelled delicious. It took everything in Worth not stop one of the servants and order himself something to go. Realizing that he was there on business, Worth pushed his hunger to the back of his mind and made his way toward the back of the restaurant where the man he'd come to see was waiting for him. The man played the shadows with a tad bit of light shining down upon him and the booth he was sitting in, eating baked ziti and taking the occasional sip of an expensive red wine. He was surrounded by hittas who were watching everything around him, ready to lay anyone or anything down that posed a threat to their boss, Baby Boy.

Once Worth had approached the table, Baby Boy looked up at him but continued to eat his delicious meal. "Sit down. Would you like something to eat? It's on me."

"No thank you. I've already eaten. I'd much rather collect and go on about my business—no offense." Worth threw up his hand, letting him know he didn't mean any disrespect by just wanting to get paid and go about his merry way. The way he saw it, once he'd done the job for him and collected, their business had concluded. Worth wasn't into making friends with the people he worked under contracts for. He preferred to keep it strictly business. That way, there weren't any misunderstandings to be had. The last thing he wanted was niggaz thinking he was going to start executing contracts on the love. Fuck that! To him, if it didn't make dollars, then it didn't make sense.

"None taken," Baby Boy said, before taking a sip of his wine. He then used his cloth napkin to wipe his mouth. Afterwards, he cleared his throat and motioned one of his goons over. He walked over to Worth and handed him a black leather bag that looked like it contained a bowling ball. There wasn't any bowling ball inside the bag though. It was loaded with cash.

"Thank you." Worth thanked Baby Boy. He turned to walk away, but Baby Boy called him back, which prompted him to turn back around to him.

"You don't wanna count that up?" Baby Boy asked him.

"No need to. I trust you want to keep the business relationship we have in good standing." Worth told him.

"Indeed I do."

Worth saluted him and went on about his business, walking towards the exit. He swayed from left to right, with the end of his duster sweeping back and forth over the floor. As he strolled along, he couldn't help thinking, *That pipsqueak is as dirty as they come. That little motherfucker paid me to kill his father, King Rich. All because he wanted his empire,* Worth shook his head. *The things people will do for fame and fortune. I tell you, family will do you dirtier than your enemies sometimes.*

"Uh!" Tyrell said as he bumped shoulders with Worth on his way inside the restaurant. He mad-dogged him and clenched his jaws, looking at his ass as if he was crazy. "Goddamn, nigga, why don't chu watch where the fuck you're going. Shit!"

Worth stopped for a second and sized him up. The men looked like they were about to get it popping inside the restaurant, but a cooler head prevailed.

"The floor's yours, tough guy," Worth said, before going about his business and headed out the exit door.

"That's what I thought, punk-ass white boy," Tyrell said and continued his stroll through the establishment. His head was on a swivel as he tried to find the man he was looking for, Baby Boy. Once he spotted him at the back of the restaurant, he made his way in his direction. He hadn't even gotten five feet within Baby Boy's table before his goons swarmed in on him and patted him down thoroughly.

Once the rest of the goons left Tyrell, Diabolic pulled out his gun and pressed it underneath his chin. Instantly, Tyrell threw his hands up in the air and swallowed the lump of fear that had formed in his throat. They were within the shadows of the restaurant so none of the patrons or employees could see what was going on with them.

"Fuck you want, nigga?" A frowned up Diabolic looked at him like he was shit at the bottom of his sneaker.

"I wanna talk to Baby Boy," Tyrell told him, frowning up at him as well. Although he was smoked out, he still held on to his gangsta. By being on crack he had lost everything but his G. It was one of the things he refused to let go of.

"What the fuck do you want with my brother?" Diabolic inquired.

"I've got some info on that shipment of coke that he lost some time ago."

Diabolic looked back at Baby Boy to see what he'd have to say about the information the dude claimed to have. Baby Boy nodded his head for Diabolic to let Tyrell go and then he took a sip of his alcohol beverage. Diabolic took his handgun from underneath Tyrell's chin and tucked it on his waistline. Baby Boy looked at Tyrell and motioned for him to have a seat at his table, which he did.

"Now, what information do you have on my shipment of cocaine?" Baby Boy asked.

"First off, is there still the fifty-k reward for anybody knowing the whereabouts of the coke and anybody involved with stealing it?"

"Yeah, the fifty large is still on the table. Now, what do you have for me?"

"What if I told you, there's two more niggaz involved in the hijacking of that shipment. Does that sound like something you may be interested in?"

Tranay Adams

"Yes. It does."

"Well, I'd like my fifty thousand dollars in all one-hundred-dollar-bills."

"Done."

Before Tyrell walked away from Baby Boy's table, he gave him Mank and Korey's names and Shavon's address. If everything checked out, then Baby Boy promised to drop Tyrell off a fifty-thousand-dollar-bag. They shook on it, and Tyrell headed for the exit. On his way out the door, Diabolic found himself trying to remember where he'd known Tyrell from. He kept seeing the crackhead's face and an old event meshing together inside his head, over and over again. It was as if his mind was rewinding and then pressing play on an old event.

Boom, boom!

Bloc, bloc, bloc, bloc!

"Bitch ass nigga, got the balls to get at me while I'm at my crib? That's yo ass, homeboy!" Tyrell swore as he and the gunman, Diabolic, moved counterclockwise behind the shielding of parked vehicles, taking shots at one another. While this was going on, a panicked Shavon was running down the steps of the house in a hurry to get to JaQuawn before he could be shot down.

Boom, boom, boom!

Bloc, bloc, bloc!

The back window of a parked Dodge Intrepid shattered and Diabolic hollered out, doubling over as he cringed. He'd been shot in the cheek. Diabolic touched his bleeding jaw and his fingertips came away bloody. He then leaned over the hood of the Dodge Intrepid, squeezing the trigger of his revolver vengefully. After he got off the last of his bullets, he took off running down the sidewalk, warm, smoking Magnum in hand.

136

Diabolic touched the old healed gunshot wound on his jaw like it wasn't a part of his face. At that moment, recognition and Tyrell's name flashed inside his head.

"I knew I knew that mothafucka!" Diabolic said aloud to no one in particular.

"What?" a frowned-up Baby Boy asked.

Diabolic leaned down and spoke into Baby Boy's ear, saying, "Yo, remember when Pops was trying to take over that block away back that that kid Tyrell was running?"

"Yeah. I remember. What's up?"

"Well, he sent me to kill the kid, but shit got botched and the nigga'z kid winded up getting killed and I winded up with a hole in my face. To make a long story short, that crackhead that just left is Tyrell, the mothafucka that shot me in the jaw." Diabolic looked back up to the exit which Tyrell had just disappeared through. He then pulled out his handgun, saying, "I'm finna go wipe that nigga out now. Save us fifty grand!"

Diabolic went to go after Tyrell but Baby Boy grabbed his arm, stopping him. "Nah, let that shit go, bro."

"Let it go?" Diabolic gave him the evil eye as he snatched his arm away. "Just why in the fuck would I do that?"

"Mannn, that nigga lost his son that night. On top of that, he's smoked the fuck out. He's a goddamn has-been, who probably wakes up every morning looking for a reason not to eat a bullet. I'd say the mothafucka has suffered enough. Soooo, let it the fuck be! You won. Hell, we won for that matter."

"Yeah, whatever, I ain't letting shit ride." Diabolic focused his attention back on the exit Tyrell had just gone through.

***

Tyrell made his way out of LaSalle's restaurant and made his way to the back of the establishment, where he saw Whitney waiting for him. He hopped into the front passenger seat and slammed the door shut, giving her the word to pull off. As she drove along, Tyrell got the crack pipe which still had crack in it, out of the glove box. He put the fire to the tip of it and inhaled harder than he ever did before, pulling as much toxic smoke into his lungs as possible. Whitney glanced back and forth between the windshield and Tyrell. A worried expression was on her face, because she'd never seen Tyrell attack a crack pipe like he was doing now.

"What's up, babe? Something on your mind?" Whitney inquired as she placed her hand gently on his thigh.

"Yeah," Tyrell said before blowing smoke into the air.

"I just saw the nigga that killed my son."

***

Jerrica, the woman that ran off with Baby Boy's car, darted back and forth across the bedroom, grabbing clothing and underwear. She'd tossed everything inside the two opened suitcases and then ran around grabbing more to toss inside the suitcases. Once she was done, she smacked the suitcases closed, leaving some of the clothing hanging out of them. She then slipped on her jacket, grabbed her car keys and the two suitcases. Jerrica flipped off the light switch and headed into the living room. She took one last look at her apartment and took a breath, hating to leave her place but realizing she really didn't have any choice in the matter. You see, Jerrica found out that the niggaz, which included her brother, that kidnapped Baby Boy were found shot the fuck up inside of their van. With them pushing up daises, little mama was sure that Baby Boy was sending his goons after her. She was sure they would find her too, especially with her still holding on to Baby Boy's car and shit. Jerrica had tried to slang that bitch, but niggaz didn't want to buy it from her, seeing as how they knew whose car it was and how much trouble it would bring should they be caught with it.

Jerrica flipped off the light switch and pulled the front door closed on her way out. She made her way down the staircase, struggling with the suitcases and nearly falling. It took her a while, but she finally managed to make it to the elevator. She pressed the down button and boarded the elevator, punching the button for the garage. Jerrica's nose scrunched up and she pinched it closed, looking around the elevator and spotting urine in the corner. Once again, some low-life mothafucka had taken the liberty to piss inside the elevator again. It was shit like this that made her glad she was moving out of the hood, and with her father's family out in New Haven, Connecticut.

The elevator doors opened and Jerrica made her way across the garage floor, heading for her car, which was parked beside Baby Boy's vehicle. Jerrica sat the suitcases down at the rear of her whip and opened the trunk. She placed her suitcases inside the trunk and slammed it shut before making her way around to the driver side door. Jerrica opened the driver's door and jumped in behind the wheel, sticking her key inside the ignition. As soon as she did, Latrell, who was wearing a bandana over the lower half of his face, slipped a length of rope over her head with his gloved hands. With a grunt, he pulled the rope tight around her neck, causing her to make a "Yuck," sound. Jerrica's eyes bulged and her mouth hung open, veins bulging on her forehead as she struggled to slip her fingers under the rope to loosen its stranglehold.

"I've got myself a fighter, huh?" Latrell said with beads of sweat oozing out of his pores and running down his face. He pulled back on the rope some more, tightening its strain on Jerrica's throat that much more. Blood clots formed in her eyes and she thrashed around wildly inside her car, kicking off one of her shoes in the process. She gagged and gagged trying to get free, and when that didn't work she started honking the horn of her car as loud as she could, hoping that someone would come to her rescue. It wasn't long before she started moving less and less, finding her life force slipping from her body. Seeing that she was slowly beginning to die, Latrell pulled back harder on the rope, which eventually caused him to snap her neck right before he officially suffocated her. Jerrica took her last breath and went rigid inside of her whip.

"Goddamn." Latrell laid his head back breathing heavily, sweat sliding down his forehead. Using the end of the black bandana he was wearing, he dabbed his wet face dry. Suddenly, his cellular rung and he pulled it out, seeing that it was Baby Boy calling him. He pressed the small green telephone on his cell phone and pressed it to his ear.

"You take care of that business we discussed earlier?" Baby Boy asked him.

Latrell looked up at Jerrica's dead eyes through the rearview mirror and confirmed the kill with his boss. "Yeah. I just finished taking care of that for you."

"Good. I've got one more thang I want chu to handle for me tonight. It's out there where you live at in Hawthorne. You'll meet Diabolic and a couple of the other guys there."

"What exactly is it you want me to do?"

"I'm not finna talk on this phone and end up on an indictment. Diabolic will explain everything to you once you get there. Now, do you have an ink pen so I can give you the address?"

"Nah, I keep everything up top," Latrell referred to his memory. "Just gemme the address."

Baby Boy gave him a very familiar address and disconnected the call before he could respond. "That's my crib. What the hell are they going to my place for? Unless...the shipment." Latrell wasn't for sure, but he believed that Mank and Korey had something to do with Baby Boy's shipment getting hit. This was because he remembered Shavon saying something about the youngstaz putting something up inside the garage she'd forgotten to inquire about. Latrell figured it had to be the shipment of coke. He wasn't for sure, but if he was a betting man then he'd bet his life on it. With that thought in his mind, Latrell hopped out of Jerrica's car and left her dead body behind inside of it. He fled to his whip which he started up and raced back to his house, hoping he'd reach his family before something tragic happened.

To Be Continued...

THE DOPEMAN'S BODYGUARD 2
Consequences & Repercussions

Submission Guideline

Submit the first three chapters of your completed manuscript to ldpsubmissions@gmail.com, subject line: Your book's title. The manuscript must be in a .doc file and sent as an attachment. Document should be in Times New Roman, double spaced and in size 12 font. Also, provide your synopsis and full contact information. If sending multiple submissions, they must each be in a separate email.

Have a story but no way to send it electronically? You can still submit to LDP/Ca$h Presents. Send in the first three chapters, written or typed, of your completed manuscript to:

LDP: Submissions Dept
Po Box 870494
Mesquite, Tx 75187

DO NOT send original manuscript. Must be a duplicate.

Provide your synopsis and a cover letter containing your full contact information.

Thanks for considering LDP and Ca$h Presents.

BOW DOWN TO MY GANGSTA

By **Ca$h**

TORN BETWEEN TWO

By **Coffee**

BLOOD STAINS OF A SHOTTA **III**

By **Jamaica**

STEADY MOBBIN **III**

By **Marcellus Allen**

BLOOD OF A BOSS **VI**

By **Askari**

LOYAL TO THE GAME **IV**

LIFE OF SIN **III**

By **T.J. & Jelissa**

A DOPEBOY'S PRAYER **II**

By **Eddie "Wolf" Lee**

IF LOVING YOU IS WRONG... **III**

LOVE ME EVEN WHEN IT HURTS **III**

By **Jelissa**

TRUE SAVAGE **VII**

By **Chris Green**

BLAST FOR ME **III**

DUFFLE BAG CARTEL **IV**

By **Ghost**

ADDICTIED TO THE DRAMA **III**

By **Jamila Mathis**

A HUSTLER'S DECEIT 3

KILL ZONE **II**

BAE BELONGS TO ME III

SOUL OF A MONSTER II

By **Aryanna**

THE COST OF LOYALTY **III**

By **Kweli**

SHE FELL IN LOVE WITH A REAL ONE **II**

By **Tamara Butler**

RENEGADE BOYS **III**

By **Meesha**

CORRUPTED BY A GANGSTA **IV**

By **Destiny Skai**

A GANGSTER'S SYN II

By **J-Blunt**

KING OF NEW YORK V

RISE TO POWER III

COKE KINGS II

By **T.J. Edwards**

GORILLAZ IN THE BAY III

De'Kari

THE STREETS ARE CALLING II

Duquie Wilson

KINGPIN KILLAZ IV

STREET KINGS 2

PAID IN BLOOD 2

Hood Rich

SINS OF A HUSTLA II

ASAD

TRIGGADALE II

Elijah R. Freeman

MARRIED TO A BOSS III

By Destiny Skai & Chris Green

KINGS OF THE GAME III

Playa Ray

SLAUGHTER GANG II

By Willie Slaughter

THE HEART OF A SAVAGE II

By Jibril Williams

FUK SHYT II

By Blakk Diamond

THE DOPEMAN'S BODYGAURD II

By Tranay Adams

<u>Available Now</u>

<u>RESTRAINING ORDER **I & II**</u>

By **CA$H & Coffee**

<u>LOVE KNOWS NO BOUNDARIES **I II & III**</u>

By **Coffee**

<u>RAISED AS A GOON I, II, III & IV</u>

<u>BRED BY THE SLUMS I, II, III</u>

<u>BLAST FOR ME I & II</u>

ROTTEN TO THE CORE I III

A BRONX TALE I, II, III

DUFFEL BAG CARTEL I II III

By **Ghost**

LAY IT DOWN **I & II**

LAST OF A DYING BREED

BLOOD STAINS OF A SHOTTA I & II

By **Jamaica**

LOYAL TO THE GAME

LOYAL TO THE GAME II

LOYAL TO THE GAME III

LIFE OF SIN I, II

By **TJ & Jelissa**

BLOODY COMMAS I & II

SKI MASK CARTEL I II & III

KING OF NEW YORK I II,III IV

RISE TO POWER I II

COKE KINGS

By **T.J. Edwards**

IF LOVING HIM IS WRONG…I & II

LOVE ME EVEN WHEN IT HURTS I II

By **Jelissa**

WHEN THE STREETS CLAP BACK I & II III

By **Jibril Williams**

A DISTINGUISHED THUG STOLE MY HEART I II & III

LOVE SHOULDN'T HURT I II III IV

RENEGADE BOYS I & II

By **Meesha**

A GANGSTER'S CODE I &, II III

A GANGSTER'S SYN

By J-Blunt

PUSH IT TO THE LIMIT

By **Bre' Hayes**

BLOOD OF A BOSS **I, II, III, IV, V**

By **Askari**

THE STREETS BLEED MURDER **I, II & III**

THE HEART OF A GANGSTA I II& III

By **Jerry Jackson**

CUM FOR ME

CUM FOR ME 2

CUM FOR ME 3

CUM FOR ME 4

An **LDP Erotica Collaboration**

BRIDE OF A HUSTLA **I II & II**

THE FETTI GIRLS **I, II& III**

CORRUPTED BY A GANGSTA I, II & III

By **Destiny Skai**

WHEN A GOOD GIRL GOES BAD

By **Adrienne**

THE COST OF LOYALTY

By Kweli

A GANGSTER'S REVENGE **I II III & IV**

THE BOSS MAN'S DAUGHTERS

THE BOSS MAN'S DAUGHTERS II

THE BOSSMAN'S DAUGHTERS III

THE BOSSMAN'S DAUGHTERS IV

THE BOSS MAN'S DAUGHTERS **V**

A SAVAGE LOVE **I & II**

BAE BELONGS TO ME I II

A HUSTLER'S DECEIT I, II, III

WHAT BAD BITCHES DO I, II, III

SOUL OF A MONSTER

By **Aryanna**

A KINGPIN'S AMBITON

A KINGPIN'S AMBITION **II**

I MURDER FOR THE DOUGH

By **Ambitious**

TRUE SAVAGE

TRUE SAVAGE II

TRUE SAVAGE **III**

TRUE SAVAGE **IV**

TRUE SAVAGE **V**

TRUE SAVAGE **VI**

By **Chris Green**

A DOPEBOY'S PRAYER

By **Eddie "Wolf" Lee**

THE KING CARTEL **I, II & III**

By **Frank Gresham**

THESE NIGGAS AIN'T LOYAL **I, II & III**

By **Nikki Tee**

GANGSTA SHYT **I II &III**

By **CATO**

THE ULTIMATE BETRAYAL

By **Phoenix**

BOSS'N UP **I , II & III**

By **Royal Nicole**

I LOVE YOU TO DEATH

By **Destiny J**

I RIDE FOR MY HITTA

I STILL RIDE FOR MY HITTA

By **Misty Holt**

LOVE & CHASIN' PAPER

By **Qay Crockett**

TO DIE IN VAIN

SINS OF A HUSTLA

By **ASAD**

BROOKLYN HUSTLAZ

By **Boogsy Morina**

BROOKLYN ON LOCK I & II

By **Sonovia**

GANGSTA CITY

By **Teddy Duke**

A DRUG KING AND HIS DIAMOND I & II III

A DOPEMAN'S RICHES

HER MAN, MINE'S TOO I, II

CASH MONEY HO'S

By **Nicole Goosby**

TRAPHOUSE KING **I II & III**

Tranay Adams

KINGPIN KILLAZ I II III

STREET KINGS

PAID IN BLOOD

By **Hood Rich**

LIPSTICK KILLAH **I, II, III**

CRIME OF PASSION I & II

By **Mimi**

STEADY MOBBN' **I, II, III**

By **Marcellus Allen**

WHO SHOT YA **I, II, III**

Renta

GORILLAZ IN THE BAY **I II**

DE'KARI

TRIGGADALE

Elijah R. Freeman

GOD BLESS THE TRAPPERS I, II, III

THESE SCANDALOUS STREETS I, II, III

FEAR MY GANGSTA I, II, III

THESE STREETS DON'T LOVE NOBODY I, II

BURY ME A G I, II, III, IV, V

A GANGSTA'S EMPIRE I, II, III, IV

THE DOPEMAN'S BODYGAURD

Tranay Adams

THE STREETS ARE CALLING

Duquie Wilson

MARRIED TO A BOSS... I II

By Destiny Skai & Chris Green

150

KINGS OF THE GAME I II

Playa Ray

SLAUGHTER GANG II

By Willie Slaughter

THE HEART OF A SAVAGE

By Jibril Williams

FUK SHYT

By Blakk Diamond

Tranay Adams

<u>BOOKS BY LDP'S CEO, CA$H</u>

<u>TRUST IN NO MAN</u>

<u>TRUST IN NO MAN 2</u>

<u>TRUST IN NO MAN 3</u>

<u>BONDED BY BLOOD</u>

<u>SHORTY GOT A THUG</u>

<u>THUGS CRY</u>

<u>THUGS CRY 2</u>

<u>THUGS CRY 3</u>

<u>TRUST NO BITCH</u>

<u>TRUST NO BITCH 2</u>

<u>TRUST NO BITCH 3</u>

<u>TIL MY CASKET DROPS</u>

<u>RESTRAINING ORDER</u>

<u>RESTRAINING ORDER 2</u>

<u>IN LOVE WITH A CONVICT</u>

<u>Coming Soon</u>

BONDED BY BLOOD 2

BOW DOWN TO MY GANGSTA

The Dopeman's Bodygaurd

CPSIA information can be obtained
at www.ICGtesting.com
Printed in the USA
LVHW050441161020
668921LV00012B/1534

9 781949 138986